THE RELUCTANT DEAD

By

NUZO ONOH

Canaan-Star Publishing

First published by Canaan-Star Publishing, United Kingdom.
www.canaan-star.co.uk

A Catalogue record for this book is available from the British Library.

ISBN: 978-1-909484-95-5

Book cover designed by Eugene Rijn R. Saratorio
Printed and bound in United Kingdom by Lightning Source, (UK) Ltd.

The stories in this book are dedicated to my beautiful mother, Caroline Onoh, the consummate story-teller; to my second mother and inspiration, Edna Izuora and to my late uncle, Sabastian Afadi, whose ghostly moonlight stories inspired a love of the supernatural and unknown in me.

ΩΩΩ

My immense gratitude to my good friend, Ted Dunphy (A.K.A Greengoalie1), without whose invaluable critique this book would never have been written in its present form. "Irish", this book is as much yours as it is mine. I thank you for everything.

About The Author

Nuzo Cambridge Onoh is a British writer of African heritage. Born in Enugu, in the Eastern part of Nigeria (formerly known as Biafra), she lived through the civil war between Biafra and Nigeria (1967 – 1970), an experience that left a strong impact on her and continues to influence her writing to date.

She attended Queen's school, Enugu, Nigeria, before proceeding to the Quaker boarding school, The Mount School, York, (England) and finally, St Andrew's Tutorial college, Cambridge, (England) from where she obtained her A' levels. Nuzo holds both a Law degree and a Masters Degree in Writing from Warwick University, (England).

She sometimes writes under the pseudonym, Alex Stranger-Onoh. She has two daughters, Candice and Jija and lives in Coventry, England.

Contents

THE RELUCTANT DEAD

THE FOLLOWER

It has been here so long...whatever It really is...but now It's inside. Somehow, It's gotten inside.

(Stephen King – IT)

Everyone said Ona was destined for great things. They said her stars blazed so strongly that the skies needed neither moon nor sun to brighten the clouds. Some people said she was blessed by the Gods; others, that she was favoured by her ancestors. The less charitable whispered that her parents must have sought the help of a witch-doctor or worse, entered an unholy union with the *Mami-water*, that fearsome mermaid that lurked beneath the murky waters of the River Niger. Otherwise, how could one girl embody all the traits of exceptional beauty, unrivalled intelligence and admirable humility? Even her name, *Ona,* was as beautiful as its translation – precious stone, diamond. When she walked, it was as if she floated on winged feet. Her voice, soft and melodious, was as sweet as the morning song of the *Okwa*, the plump nightingale. And when she smiled, her pearly teeth flashed as if they were polished with the superior *Nzu* chalk which Mama Shedrach moulded and baked in her backyard fireplace every *Oye* market day.

Ona's father, Agu, was the envy of his peers. They nick-named him *"Papa Ego",* father of money, because of his pot of gold, his only daughter, Ona. Everyone knew that when Ona graduated from her teachers' training college, she would be scooped up by the wealthiest suitor in the land. Already, the villagers had witnessed several big cars frequenting Agu's modest bungalow within the past months. Agu's spinster sister, Chika, that incorrigible *Amibo*, who wouldn't give up her livelihood of gossiping even if Jesus promised her Angel Michael in marriage, told everyone who cared to listen that over six suitors here vying for Ona's hand in marriage, including a politician, a lawyers and even a footballer all the way from England. Chika said that the footballer had promised to pay Ona's dowry in pound sterling! She quoted a sum that boggled the minds of the villagers. The wizards in mathematics did the conversion and came up with a figure that would buy Agu a couple of Mercedes Benz cars and even build him a one-storey house with an upstairs balcony as well! Was it any wonder he gladly answered to the name *"Papa Ego"*, what with a daughter who was a guaranteed money-machine. That wretched gossip, Chika, even hinted that Agu might soon take a chieftaincy title and become an *Ozo*, a village peer, wearing the coveted elephant's ivory amulets and an eagle's feather in his cap. Indeed, if one looked closely, a person would surely see the smug twist in Agu's plump lips, the slight swagger in his steps and a general demeanour that proclaimed to all and sundry, "I am a very contented man, favoured by my *chi* and blessed by my ancestors!"

Until the day Ona disappeared.

It happened on the morning of her eighteenth birthday, the day Agu was expected to announce his daughter's engagement to the footballer from England, John Udo. Yes; there had been some truth after all in Chika's rumour-mongering. The footballer had indeed bested his rivals despite their impressive university degrees and superior professions. In the end, money screamed louder than class and the Nigerian *Naira* had been no match for the British Pounds. But all that came to a halt on the morning Ona walked out of her father's compound to collect her birthday gown from the seamstress's shop at Ogbete market. It was a mere twenty minute's ride on the *Okada*, that ubiquitous motorbike-taxi that ferried people across the busy town of Enugu, with its congested roads and house-choked streets.

But by the time the shrine rooster shepherded his harem of clucking hens into their thatched coop at sundown, Agu, like the infamous Cain, bore the stamp of a cursed fate on the deep ridges across his forehead, the stooped slope of his shoulders and the hopeless, haunted look in his kola-red eyes. He would neither speak nor eat. His two sons, Umunnakwe and Ike, tried to coax him back to the land of the living with words of faith…hope, even as they scoured the lands and rivers for their missing sister. The footballer, John Udo, who was yet to be an official son-in-law, collapsed from shock and withdrew from the public eyes for several days following the tragedy, nursing his grief in solitude. Nonetheless, he poured his impressive wealth into the search, bribing policemen, paying witch-doctors, donating to prayer warriors from numerous Pentecostal churches and taking out daily television and newspaper advertisements.

All to no avail.

It was as if Ona had vanished from existence; as if she had never crossed the spirit land of the ancestors to begin her latest reincarnation on *Amadioha*'s earth. The Divisional Police Officer, known as the "Devil Police Orange" on account of his weight and light skin, demanded money to buy black-market petrol for the police vehicles used in the search for Ona. And John Udo, that fortuitous milk-cow from England, paid … and paid; while Agu, the heartbroken father, stared …and stared.

At nothing.

Until the day he stared at the decomposed corpse of a young woman found at a cassava farm and recognised the mud-stained white beads on the thin braids of his daughter's hair and the polished nails that remained pink and groomed in the rotting carcass of what was once his beautiful precious stone.

******

Afam knew that he was drunk; very drunk. With that clarity peculiar to the highly intoxicated, he recognised that his unsteady gait and trembling hands were unsuited for his job. Not that his supervisor would sack him for being drunk on the job anyway. *Idiot hospital was lucky to have him in the first place. After all, how many graduates would agree to work in a morgue, especially on the night shift?* Unless of course, they were like him, desperate and destitute and ready to do anything for the money to pay the black-market fee for an Italian visa, so he could get away from this God-forsaken country.

Morgue duty was a soul-killer, a strength-stealer that unman-ed a warrior and ruined the heart of a lion. Afam didn't consider himself a coward. Yet, the morgue had badly dented his man-heart. He had eventually adjusted to washing and embalming cold clammy bodies in the daytime, when the hospital corridors bustled with activity and sunlight streamed through the dusty overhead glass windows. Then, he could look at the lifeless bodies and handle them with the automated indifference of a callous butcher. They might as well be the Christmas ram he butchered every year at his family's compound for all he cared.

But night-time was a different story. Night-time was when the unwritten rules of the morgue applied, rules that sent the chills down his spine and left his limbs as weak as a day old foal's. The rules had been handed down to him on the first day he reported for duty, barely two weeks gone. The elderly supervisor had talked him through the job, explaining the processes and policies as he led Afam across the vast cold room, littered with corpses of both sexes in different stages of undress and decomposition.

'Best bit about our job is that we get to keep any jewellery or money we find on our guests,' the supervisor had said with a wink, rubbing his hands together, his nails as filthy as the blood-spattered apron he donned. *Guests!* That of course was rule number one, as the supervisor proceeded to explain in a grave voice. One must never refer to the bodies as corpses. It was disrespectful to them. They didn't take kindly to being referred to in such undignified terms, not even in jest.

'Don't forget to ask their permission first before undressing or cleaning them, ok? They get very angry if you don't ask, especially the women. I'm sure you can understand, eh?' Supervisor laughed, his teeth rotten, showing a kola-stained brown beneath fleshy lips. Afam did not understand but he nodded all the same, his smile as strained as his heart beneath his bony ribs. *Better to humour the idiot man till he settled in the job.* 'Don't worry, though,' continued Supervisor, pulling a dirty white sheet over the exposed breasts of a female corpse that had been brought in that morning. Afam wished the supervisor would cover the dead woman's face as well, not just her breasts. He was petrified of the peeling skin, the putrid stench of decay, the yawning mouth tunnelling into an endless black cave and the mottled lids that seemed as if they would fly open in an instant. For a brief second, Afam wondered what she must have looked like in life. Only her bead-encased thin braids and beautifully manicured nails gave a hint of beauty and youth. *Such a waste!*

'Don't worry, my boy. Day duty isn't too bad.' Supervisor's voice broke into Afam's musings, dragging back his wandering thoughts. 'It's when you're on night duty that you have to observe the rules. You must…'

'Night duty?' Afam broke into Supervisor's speech, his voice pitched like a woman's. 'No one said anything to me about night duty at the interview.'

The supervisor laughed, his voice laced with unrepressed glee. 'My boy, everyone does night duty here, from the doctors to the nurses, the cleaners to the security guards. It's a hospital after all, you know. Sickness and death don't choose what hour to afflict the human race.' His voice held a mocking tinge.

Afam groaned inwardly, cursing his wretched luck. He was seriously beginning to rethink the job, Italy or no Italy.

'How many times in a week will I have to do night duty?' Afam asked, his voice rising with a feeling he was loath to recognise as panic. *Chineke!* God our creator! He had been cheated! Bastard medical director should have disclosed everything at the job interview. He would have definitely questioned the salary had he known.

'It's a one week on and one week off shift,' Supervisor said. 'As a new starter, you will do the day shift for two weeks. That will give you time to familiarise yourself with the guests as they come and go. Then in your third week, you will do the night shift and from then, it's one week days and one week nights in rotating shifts.' Supervisor paused to look into Afam's stricken expression. 'Why? Are you afraid, my boy?' His voice was suddenly gentle.

Afam felt shame and pride in equal proportion. He shook his head, squaring his shoulders.

'Of course I'm not afraid,' he snapped. 'Why should I be?' It was more a statement of self-bolstering than it was a question. But Supervisor took it as the latter.

'Indeed my boy! Why should you be afraid? There's nothing to fear from our guests as long as you obey the rules.' Supervisor placed an overly-familiar arm across

Afam's shoulders. 'As I said, never call them by any other name than guests or even better, friends. Secondly, always ask their permission before touching them. And before I forget, they enjoy being talked to as you embalm them, okay?' Again, Afam nodded. 'The other three rules are simple and as I said, they apply only on night shift. The most important night rule is to always knock on the door before you enter the mortuary; three knocks at least, okay?'

It wasn't okay. Not by a long shot.

'Why three knocks? In fact, why any knock at all?' Afam asked, beginning to suspect the supervisor was taking the mickey.

'Shhh...keep your voice down before you disturb their sleep.' The supervisor steered him out of the morgue, his hand firm on Afam's shoulder. 'Listen my boy, you have to show some respect,' Supervisor admonished, his voice cold. Gone was the earlier affability. Afam looked into the steely glint in his rheumy eyes and felt a sudden chill in the narrow hot corridor of the hospital. *Creepy bastard!* 'You ask me why you have to knock at all. Well, let me ask you; would you be happy if someone barged into your house without knocking, eh?' Supervisor didn't wait for Afam's response. 'I think not. Well, the mortuary may not be their home but it is their hotel, okay? It's their temporary abode till they are taken to their final resting place. So, as long as they are our guests, we will treat them with the respect they deserve, okay?' This time, Supervisor waited for Afam's slow nod before continuing. 'Good. Now as for the second night rule. You must never sit facing the room. Once you enter, always turn your chair to face the door and no matter what you hear, never look behind you, okay?'

Definitely not okay in Afam's book. *Hell no!*

'What do you mean no matter what I hear behind me?' Afam didn't bother to lower his voice. 'What the hell am I supposed to hear?' The supervisor gave a deep sigh and paused for several seconds, staring steadily into Afam's face, his brows dipped, his eyes, speculative. He seemed suddenly to be struggling with the words he had been using with reckless abandon ever since Afam reported for duty that morning.

'Well…how do I explain? Let's see…Okay. Say you're in your bedroom. You're lying on your bed. Your side starts hurting from lying on that side too long. Or perhaps, your arm goes numb from lying on it. So, you decide to turn to another side. Or say you have a bad dream and cry out in your sleep. You wouldn't want anyone watching you as you sleep, would you now? Well it's the same with our guests.'

'Rubbish! They're dead. With all due respect sir, they can't get their arms numb or have nightmares.'

'How do you know? Have you walked in their shoes, eh?' Supervisor's voice was laced with scorn. 'That's the problem with you university people. You think because you know books and have a degree you know everything. Well, let me tell you my boy, I have been in this job for twenty-seven years now, longer than you have been in this world. I have seen things you would never comprehend in your life. So, when I tell you that our guests have nightmares, then take it from me, I know what I'm talking about. Now, just listen and do as you're told, okay?'

This time, Afam neither nodded nor spoke. He'd finally figured out the supervisor's problem. *The man was jealous of the fact that he was a university graduate*. He wanted to exercise power, demean Afam even more than he was already demeaned by taking the morgue job in the first place. God knew that nothing would have made him stoop to such a job if he hadn't spent the last three years since graduation searching fruitlessly for a job. His friend in Italy had told him things were much easier there if only he could get himself a visa. Once there, he would marry an Italian girl and get his Italian passport. Then he would start exporting cars back to Nigeria just like his friend and eventually build himself a mansion in his village. No one would deny him a chieftaincy title then; possibly, an *Ozo* peerage as well despite his youth. Afam had it all planned out. Italy was where the money was but first he had to save the *Naira* to pay for his visa. The mortuary job was the first job offer he'd had in over three years and now he had this buffoon of a boss to contend with on top of everything else.

'The final and most important rule is to recite the Lord's Prayer to our guests before you leave at 6am,' Supervisor continued. 'That's everything for now. For your sake, I hope you observe all the rules, as I wouldn't want to be responsible should anything happen to you.'

'Like what?' Afam's voice had a sneer he barely bothered to conceal. 'What'll happen to me if I don't observe these rules?'

'How should I know?' Supervisor shrugged. 'I've told you everything I know. The rest is up to you. I have to leave now. Report tomorrow at 6am prompt and don't forget to collect your work pack from the store-room, okay?'

******

All that had taken place almost three weeks ago. Afam had done two weeks day shift with little or no trouble. His initial squeamishness had soon disappeared to the point that he was even able to assist in the embalming of the dead woman with the beaded braids and groomed nails. He had to admit that the supervisor knew his job despite his superstitious drivel. Afam had watched the supervisor clean the girl's body and orifices with strong chemicals, taking great care to log in all cuts, bruises and discolorations in the embalming report book. (Thankfully, there had been no jewellery or money to steal from the poor girl. It didn't feel right to him watching Supervisor steal property from the dead. So far, Afam had politely declined taking his share of the loot, which seemed to displease the supervisor, who was happy enough keeping everything).

Next, Supervisor did the arterial embalming with undiluted formaldehyde, due to the decomposed state of the girl's body. The medical examiner had removed the internal organs during autopsy and Supervisor had injected cavity fluids into her torso before gluing her eyelids together and suturing her mouth with suture strings. By the time thick cover make-up had been applied, hiding all the bruises and discoloration, Afam had to admit that the poor girl looked almost as good as her picture he'd seen in the newspapers.

She was the missing fiancée of that famous British footballer, John Udo. The autopsy report confirmed Supervisor's theory that she had been raped and then strangled before being dumped in the cassava farm, almost a hundred kilometres from her village. Little wonder it had taken her family so long to find her. The police were still searching for her murderer - *fat chance of them catching anyone, what with their corruption and incompetence. God! How he loathed this damned country!* Still, Afam hoped for the poor girl's sake that the police would for once, defy expectations and actually bring the evil murderer to justice. Whoever the animal was that committed this vile crime, deserved to have a burning tyre put round his neck and lynched by a mob.

In the two weeks of day shift, Afam had neither knocked nor prayed nor asked any corpses' permission to clean their rotten bodies for them. *He'd be damned if he sunk to that illiterate Supervisor's level and fell prey to ignorant superstitions. If anything, the so-called "guests" should be falling on their rotten knees, praying for him and thanking him for sorting out their putrid carcasses.* He had learnt to ignore Supervisor's accusing looks and disapproving clucks in the first week he'd worked alongside the man. He had worked mostly alone in his second week and had to admit the job was pretty easy. In fact, he had finished reading two novels on the job in just one week, a new record for him; anything to kill the boredom and speed up time.

But then came yesterday or rather, yester-night, his first night duty at the morgue and the reason for his present state of inebriation. *Chineke!* Even thinking about it now as he stumbled along the lit-up streets of Enugu, gave him the Harmattan chills…right through to his bones. *The silence!* That terrible unearthly silence that seemed never-ending - oppressive, chilling. The tingling feeling in his back; a crawling sensation at the base of his neck; the certainty that someone was staring at him, that those dozens of dead eyes were boring into his back through their glued lids. The bright overhead florescent bulb kept flickering all night till NEPA, the wretched Nigerian Electric Power Authority (better known by the acronym, "Never Expect Power Always") finally took away the power, plunging the room in a terrible darkness that threatened to rob Afam of his sanity!

He had abandoned all pretence at bravery and stumbled out of the cold room into the equally dark but warm corridor, caring little whether or not the sound of crashing chair and slamming door awoke the slumbering "guests". He just wanted to get as far as possible from the God-forsaken place. And he would have continued running had the hospital Generator not kicked back the failed electricity supply, flooding the corridor in blinding but welcoming light.

Dear Jesus in His sweet heavens! Had he ever taken light for granted, fool that he was? Never again! After tonight, he would never grumble about his girlfriend's habit of sleeping with the lamp on; never, ever! *Chineke!* He wouldn't be surprised if he too started sleeping with the lights on after the night's awful experience.

Afam lingered in the corridor for several minutes after the lights came on again, staring at the shut door of the morgue, trying to summon the courage to return to what was beginning to be the scariest place on earth for him. *For God's sake, what could possibly happen to him in there? Hadn't he spent the last two weeks in that same room without any problems? What the hell was so different about night time anyway, apart from his stupidity in following the pathetic night-shift rules and turning his back to the corpses?* But Supervisor already had the chair facing the door before he'd reported for duty and he just didn't bother doing otherwise. Well, he'd be damned if he allowed the supervisor's superstitious drivel to get to him. *Come on, man!*

Squaring his shoulders, Afam proceeded in a leisurely saunter towards the shut white door with the filthy stains that could well be blood for all he knew. *Who gave a fuck?* Supervisor wasn't the most hygienic man in God's universe and the blasted guests wouldn't be dying from any infections soon, would they? Neither were they likely to be up in arms against him for waking them up in his mad rush from the room following the power failure.

Still….

His traitorous heart wouldn't stop pounding as he drew closer to the door. With each step he took, it felt as if his heart would plunge right through his stomach and hit the hard cement floor of the corridor. His breath was coming in quick busts and he could feel his head expanding and contracting in steady succession. Then, he was standing right in front of the door, tugging his thick sweater over his hips for the third time, nodding his head again and again like a grey lizard, hearing his breathing, hard and loud against the muted hum of the Generator. *You can do this, man. Come on!*

He placed his sweaty hand on the brass knob of the door and did a quick sign of the cross. Taking a deep breath, he pushed open the door with a forceful shove…and entered the morgue.

Was it his imagination or did he hear something that sounded like mice…no…scuttling feet, at the far right-hand corner of the room? It was the side where that poor girl, Ona, rested in silent repose in the industrial size glass freezer, awaiting collection for her funeral the next day. Afam stared intently at that section of the morgue, feeling the sudden tensing of his shoulders and the fierce dipping of his brows. The shadows seemed to gather in thick clouds in that section of the room despite the florescent lighting. Afam forced his feet towards the corpse; *not too close now.*

He stopped in mid-motion, his heart thudding, his legs almost collapsing beneath him. Someone was standing behind him! *Oh God! Holy Mary mother of God! He* could feel the cold air at the back of his neck - someone's breath - whispery, faint… but so cold; a heavy presence behind him, waiting…bearing down…

Afam turned, letting out a shout, pushing at invisible air with his outstretched arms. He glanced around the room, his eyes wild, terror coursing through his veins. He stumbled back towards the door, panting, feeling his skin crawl under a damp sheet of cold sweat. *He really had to get a grip on himself, shrieking like a woman and scaring himself shitless*. But he had been so sure…could have sworn there was someone…*something...*behind him. He hadn't imagined the breathing, the sudden chill raising the hair at the back of his neck. *Still, could have been a draft from the noisy air-conditioner*. He looked again at the corner shrouded in shadows, at that female corpse that had fascinated him from the first day.

This time, he felt the sudden swelling of his head as he struggled to reign in his terror. *What the hell! Were his eyes playing tricks on him or hadn't Ona's arms been folded beneath the white sheet that shrouded her embalmed body? So why was her left arm now hanging down her side and her left foot exposed to the naked eye? And what on Amadioha's earth was that phosphorus mass that hung around the corpse like a thin veil of mist, swirling, rising and falling like a living, breathing presence?*

Afam's took several deep breaths, trying to steady the erratic tempo of his heart. *All he needed now was to have a heart attack and join the rest of the blasted guests in their icy chamber. Fat lot of good that will do him and his Italian visa. Idiot man!* Brows furrowed, he tried to recall how the bodies had been arranged before NEPA disrupted the electricity supply. Steeling himself, he forced his gaze to take in the rest of the vast room, resting briefly on each of the corpses on the exposed slabs and open freezers.

There was Chief Micah, the fat diabetic who had been a resident for the past week. Micah had been a wealthy trader and his family were planning a befitting funeral, if only his four wives would reach a consensus on the arrangements. In the meantime, Micah would remain in the morgue for as long as it took them to sort out their domestic differences and get on with his funeral. They could afford to pay the hefty daily morgue tariffs anyway.

Afam felt his fear slowly subside as he recalled the mundane in that cold chamber of horrors.

Next to Micah was the old woman....Afam couldn't remember her name but they said her son was one of the doctors in the hospital. Afam didn't really know most of the other corpses in the room. They had arrived while he'd been off duty over the weekend. Most of them rested on open slabs. Afam could always tell the status of each corpse by their appearance and location in the morgue. The affluent bodies were treated with expensive chemicals and make up and placed in the drawer-freezers for better preservation. The destitute ones were mostly abandoned on the exposed metal slabs after the most basic treatment, till they were either claimed by their families or dumped unceremoniously at the holding bay at the rear of the hospital, to await mass burial at the state-run cemetery. Afam was glad that poor girl, Ona, was leaving the next morning. She deserved better than the wretched morgue.

He returned to his table, his steps reluctant, pulling up his plastic chair from the linoleum floor. With slow deliberation, he turned it facing the morgue and its lifeless guests. *Fuck the idiot rules!* No way was he turning his back to the room again. Over his dead body! *Dead body... ha!* Afam barked a mirthless laugh. He got a brush and cleared up the pieces of broken glass from the floor, feeling slight embarrassment at the brittle evidence of his earlier cowardice. He returned to his chair and sat down, allowing his eyes to roam the room. He found it was easier facing the lifeless bodies now, stamping their presence in his mind till they became ordinary once again…normal…losing their ability to instil fear and horror. He would make sure he brought in a torch tomorrow night; perhaps, even borrow his cousin's transistor radio. Nothing like a noisy radio to banish the oppressive terrors of night-time silence.

The rest of the night had passed in relative peace, aided by the steady humming of the Generator and noisy air-condition unit. The only break from the norm was when a new corpse was wheeled in sometime around 3am, a young man who had died from a motorbike accident. Afam had tried to keep the attendants talking for as long as he could, just to have some company. The new corpse somehow frightened him more than the rest. He guessed it was because the man was too close to his age and reminded him of his own mortality. There was something very unsettling about the ruined and bloody body, the bashed-in head and swollen features. Afam had simply logged in his details and wheeled him to the far corner of the morgue for the supervisor to embalm in the morning. *Jesus would return to earth before he touched that wrecked body.* Instead, Afam covered the corpse with a white sheet – *Why on earth do they insist on using these bloody white sheets which heightened rather than lessened the macabre of death?* He thought. Left to him, the bodies would simply be covered with bright colourful wrappers, normal items of everyday clothing which they had probably used in their lifetime. He certainly wouldn't want to be covered in an idiot white sheet when he died.

As the sun finally broke through the night clouds at dawn, replacing the artificial yellow light of the florescent bulb with its brilliant and welcoming blaze, Afam gave a silent prayer of thanks. *He had got through his first night-shift at the morgue!* He had survived what had been an unconscious burden on his mind ever since he started the job. The rest was easy now. Bleary-eyed, he stumbled out of the room when Supervisor turned up for the day-shift. He'd barely bothered to respond to the man's "good morning my boy", too drained by his night vigil in the company of the dead. He took an *Okada* taxi back to the small room he shared with his girlfriend, Uzo, a hair-dresser with breasts large enough to feed ten babies. Afam liked big breasts in women, even better than big butts. A man could sleep forever on the chest of a big-busted woman. He wished Uzo would still be at home. He needed her more than he'd ever needed anyone in his life after his first night-shift work at the morgue. *Chineke!* He was so tired…absolutely knackered. He could literally sleep forever, the way he felt.

Uzo had been at home when he returned, but only just. She was running late for work and hardly had enough time to ask how his night went without waiting to hear his answer. She had a she-devil for a boss and hair-dressers were like flies on a rotten corpse these days. It wouldn't be difficult to replace Uzo if she was found wanting in any way. *Still… it wouldn't have killed her to pay him a bit more attention.* For someone who'd been harping on marriage for over a year, she was sure making little effort to get him on board.

Afam washed himself in the little out-house which stank of stale urine all year round. Afterwards, he retired to their stuffy room above the barber's shop and crashed out on their double bed. In no time, he was out of the ruckus and mayhem that was the urban jungle of his city-centre street.

******

It was the cold that woke him up, a numbing chill that seemed to have crept into every pore in his weary body, leaving his teeth rattling and his body shuddering. *Chineke!*

Was he coming down with malaria or God forbid, typhoid? *God!* The last time he'd felt this cold was the first day he'd worked at the heavily air-conditioned morgue. Supervisor had forgotten to tell him to bring a thick jumper to work and he had turned up in his plain short-sleeves and trousers. He'd spent the whole day shivering and praying for the shift to come to an end so he would escape into the wonderful warmth of God's sunshine.

Afam stumbled out of bed and rushed over to the louvred window facing the busy street below. With cold-numb fingers, he fumbled with the louvre handle till he pushed the panes wide open. Instantly, the warm air from the mid-day sun poured into the room, warming his body and bringing some feeling back to his numb limbs. Such was his relief that he wanted to bolt naked from the room to soak up the warm sunshine outside. *What the hell was the matter with him? Whatever it was, he didn't want it. He needed his health to remain in its usual perfect state for his job. Bad enough working with the dead without feeling like them.* He stretched himself, yawning widely as he returned to his bed with the metal frame work and mosquito net.

This time, Afam's startled scream could be heard in the street below his open window. He literally flew out of his bed like a pebble fired from a boy's catapult and bumped his right knee against Uzo's make-up table by the window. *Chineke! Jesus! What the hell was that?* Rubbing his aching joint, Afam stared at the bed, his eyes as wide as an owl's, his brows furrowed. His movements tentative, he reached out his right hand towards the black metal frame of the bed. Again, he let out an involuntary shout, withdrawing his hand like one stung by a scorpion. The bed was freezing, an iciness that was beyond anything he'd ever known. *Chei!* It was a miracle he hadn't frozen to death sleeping in that icy coffin! But what the fuck was wrong with the bed? How on earth could it get that cold in the middle of a hot tropical afternoon?

Then the smell hit him, a terrible smell that was as familiar to him as it was strange to his cramped room. It was a smell he had inhaled for over two weeks, a cloying smell of decayed meat, rotten eggs and funk. It was the smell of death, corruption and formaldehyde. *Dear God in heaven! Holy Mary Mother of God! He had brought the mortuary back home with him!*

Like a man deranged, Afam began gathering his work clothes, the thick red sweater and black trousers, the sturdy black boots and grey woolly socks, even his vest and underpants. He chucked the lot into the plastic bucket he had used to wash himself just that very morning. His movements were frenzied, even manic, as he carried the bucket and its unwanted contents out of the room. The stale air in the corridor hit him with welcoming warmth as he dumped the bucket by the staircase. Breathing hard, he returned to the open door of his room, inhaled….

And gagged!

Tufia! God forbid! The smell was even stronger, more pungent, as if the morgue itself had been transported to his little room! *It just wasn't possible!* And the chill! The room felt like a freezer. He might as well be one of the corpses in the morgue, the way things were.

All thought of sleep now vanished, Afam quickly dressed up and left the room, averting his eyes from the abandoned bucket at the top of the stairs as he fled from the house and its weirdness. He would head over to his cousin's flat at the other end of the street and wait out the rest of the afternoon till Uzo returned from work. Hopefully by then, the smell would have disappeared out of the open window, with the inexplicable chill.

'The most important night rule is to always knock on the door before you enter at night... three knocks at least, okay?'

From nowhere, Supervisor's oily voice insinuated itself into Afam's head, causing him to stumble as he walked the busy street choked with street hawkers and *Fulani* beggars. *What on earth was the matter with him today? Why was he falling to pieces just from one night-*

shift? He cursed the idiot Supervisor loudly, not caring if people thought him crazy, talking to himself in a public place. *Creepy bastard! Filling his head with all that crap about fucking "guests" and their bloody rules!*

Still…

Afam found himself looking over his shoulders and hurrying his steps along the dusty path bordering the asphalt road. *God! But it was bloody cold! Chei!*

Arriving at his cousin's flat, Afam was relieved to find Udoka at home. But his joy vanished as soon as Udoka spoke.

'*Chei!* My brother! What kind of smell is this you have, eh?' Udoka screwed up his nose, a look of disgust in his handsome features! Afam felt his heart begin to race. *It wasn't possible! He'd changed into clean clothes. He'd had a wash too. Hell! He'd even walked the distance to Udoka's flat in the inexplicable cold breeze of the street, considering the blazing sun. There shouldn't be any smell on him. He certainly couldn't smell anything.*

'What do you mean?' Afam's voice was aggressive. 'What smell are you talking about?' Afam shoved his cousin aside as he stepped into Udoka's living-room and plonked himself on the red fabric sofa.

'You tell me, man!' Udoka shot back, still standing by the open door, his hand now covering his nose. 'Why on earth didn't you have a wash after working at that blasted morgue? God! You stink worse than a corpse! Shit!'

'I had a wash… I even changed my clothes. I don't know what you say you can smell. I can't smell a thing'

'Then your nose must be blocked with catarrh or else you've become too used to the smell of dead bodies to notice that you now smell like one.' Udoka began to open all the windows in his flat before turning on the overhead electric fan. Afam shivered, feeling the chill even more than when he'd been in the street.

'Man, it's freezing in here!' Udoka rushed to switch off the fan he'd only just turned on. 'What kind of Harmattan cold is this we're having in the middle of July, I ask you?'

'Udo… I am worried.' Afam's voice was barely audible as he stared at his cousin, his dark pupils reflecting the sudden terror in his heart. It wasn't just him anymore. Udoka could smell the same thing that had sent him fleeing from his room. Except that now, he couldn't smell it anymore. And this inexplicable chill…what on earth was happening to him? 'Udo… sit down, please,' Afam leaned forward to grab his cousin's wrist, pulling him down by him. But no sooner had Udoka sat down than he jumped right off the sofa again, staring at Afam as if he had grown horns and tails.

'Afam, I swear something is wrong with you; I'm not joking, man. You really, *really* stink and being near you is like being inside a fridge.'

'That's what I'm trying to tell you,' Afam's voice held a frightened intensity. 'Udo, ever since I returned from night-shift today, this smell and chill has followed me everywhere. That's why I left my room and came here. Worst thing is that I can't even smell anything anymore. But somehow, you can. All I know is that I'm now constantly cold. I don't know what it is or what to do about it. Udo, what do you think is happening to me?'

Udoka shrugged. 'Man, you work in a hospital. Maybe you should see a doctor straight away. I really think you've picked up something in that place. I'm not the least bit surprised, tell you the truth. What normal person would want to wash up dead bodies anyway?' Udoka shook his head, heading off to his kitchen. 'Let me get you some Nivaquine in case you're coming down with malaria, alright?'

'No…thanks. I don't need Nivaquine,' Afam's face creased in a weary smile. Udoka was an incorrigible hypochondriac with every medicine under the sky in his kitchen cupboard. Little wonder he was still unmarried despite his good looks, when most of his age-grade were already fathers. Probably convinced he would catch herpes from kissing a girl or Aids from sleeping with one. He only wished Udoka had some medicine in his cupboard for this bizarre affliction he was going through.

Afam stood up to leave. 'But you're right. I need to see a doctor without delay. Thanks, Bro. I'll tell you how it goes.' Afam headed to the still open door of Udoka's flat.

The walk back to his house was a nightmare. He was aware of people screwing up their noses as they brushed past him in the street. Someone even cursed him for the stinky pig he was! *Him, Afam Okeke, who had never missed a daily wash in his life!* The sooner he saw a doctor and sorted out this problem the better he'd feel.

The bucket was still where he had left it by the staircase in the corridor with its unwanted contents. Afam stooped to pick up the clothes he'd been in a hurry to discard, his thick red jumper and black trousers. He sniffed them. It was as he suspected. They smelled normal, slightly of disinfectant and aftershave, certainly nothing like the vile odour that had driven him from his room and followed him all the way to Udoka's flat and back, going by people's reactions in the street. He carried the bucket into the room and put it under the table. Then he went towards the bed and stood by, staring at it for several seconds. Finally, stretching out his hand, he placed a tentative fore-finger on the black metal frame.

Nothing...

The bed was as normal as normal could be, temperature, tepid. Whatever had made it icy earlier on had gone. Afam was beginning to suspect he was the cause. Hadn't Udoka said that being near him was like being near a fridge? And this persistent chill that clung to him like a second shirt, causing him bouts of involuntary shivers. Well, the doctor will soon sort it out, whatever it was.

In no time, Afam was dressed again in his work clothes, even packed a torch. *Pity about the radio.* He'd forgotten to ask Udoka for it in the entire hullabaloo about the damned smell. He could survive one more night at the morgue without it.

The doctor took his temperature and blood pressure and both were normal. But the man wore a green mask over his mouth and nose throughout the examination. He asked Afam a lot of questions about his personal hygiene and bowel movements and made notes. But one thing he did comment on was the condition of Afam's skin, which he said was abnormally cold, even icy to the touch. He sent Afam for a blood and Urine test and asked him to return the next week when the results would be ready. In the meantime, he prescribed Nivaquine and Ampiclox antibiotics, just in case it was malaria or typhoid fever. Afam thanked the man and left. *He would have been better taking Udoka's medicine for all the help the doctor had been with his stupid green mask*. He glanced at his watch – only 2.15pm. He still had over three hours to kill till his night-shift. Might as well go home. No way was he hanging around in the miserable hospital canteen till 6pm.

Uzo was already home when he opened the door to their room. She started to smile…then her face froze and screwed up in the vile expression that was beginning to be familiar to Afam.

'Huhh! Where have you been? You stink worse than a pit toilet. Go and have a wash before you come in here.' She turned to open the louvre panes of the window but found they were already open. She hissed in exasperation.

'Uzo, I've already had a wash,' Afam's voice was weary. He didn't know how many more times he would have to explain himself to people. The way things were, he might as well become a hermit or relocate to the bloody morgue where his smell wouldn't be an issue at all. 'I've just been to see a doctor. I seem to be coming down with something which the doctor can't figure out yet. He sent me for some tests. Hopefully, it will all be sorted out by next week when the results are out.'

'I hope you don't expect me to cope with that smell for a whole week,' Uzo sounded anything but sympathetic.

'You'll have to find somewhere to stay till you get rid of it.'

Again, Afam wondered why he was still with the woman whom his cousin and friends loathed, mainly because she was six years older than him. But he knew the answer. Her breasts; and the fact that she'd more or less, been his meal ticket through his years of unemployment. Even the rent was paid by her. Otherwise, her self-centredness and bossiness were enough to send any sane man running the opposite direction. One thing he was determined never to do, though, was marry her, despite all her hints and pressure. Now he had a job, he planned to move into his own place as soon as he got his first salary. No doubt some people would call him callous but he didn't give a damn. They should come and spend a week in Uzo's company before making any judgement on him.

'I'll put some stuff in a bag and get going. I'll stay at my cousin's place till it's sorted out. I'll text you when everything's okay.' Afam started packing his things, feeling a slow anger building up in him. Uzo's nonchalance hardened his resolve to make the move a permanent one. *God knows he won't be feeling any guilt when he receives his pay in less than two weeks' and rents his own place. She could go find herself some other fool to marry and bully.*

Udoka was surprised to see Afam back so soon but angered by Uzo's actions.

'Of course you can stay with me, Bro. We're family, aren't we? Blood is thicker than any fucking smell. You'll see; everything will be just fine once the results are out. Did you collect your prescription from the chemist?' Afam shook his head. He already knew where Udoka was headed.

'Here, you can take the prescription and keep the medicine for yourself,' he handed over the prescription to Udoka, unable to suppress a smile at the ecstatic expression on his cousin's face. More loot for his medicine horde, no doubt. But he was grateful to his cousin; very grateful. Not many people would take him in smelling the way he did, even though he could smell nothing. *But he knew what he smelled like*. He had smelled it when it first attached itself to him that morning. *God! Was it only this morning that everything happened? It felt like a thousand years already!* That was when he began to drink, after the self-pity and depression hit him. And by the time his mobile's alarm function beeped for his second night shift at the morgue, Afam knew that he was drunk, very drunk. But who gave a fuck? They were bloody lucky to have him working at their stinking morgue anyway. *Bloody fucking lucky!*

******

'My boy, you've got a follower,' Supervisor said as soon as Afam stumbled into the morgue later that evening.

'A follower? Who?' Afam glance behind. 'There's no one following me.' Supervisor shook his head sadly.

'I warned you about the night rules, didn't I? But clearly you didn't obey. And now, you've got yourself a follower and only God knows how long he or she will become your shadow.' Again, Supervisor shook his head and started pulling off his apron in readiness to leave. Afam felt the shivers run through his body, from his head to his toes. He felt a chill beyond anything he could describe. The fuzziness cleared from his head in an instant, replaced by a terror that threatened to send him bolting from the corpse-littered room.

'*Oga*...boss, what do you mean? What follower are you talking about?' Afam's voice had an edge of desperation as he clutched the supervisor by his sleeves, all bravado gone.

There was smug satisfaction in the supervisor's face, nonetheless, tinged with pity.

'A follower is one of our guests,' he replied, nodding towards the white-shrouded bodies in the morgue. 'I smelt them on you as soon as you entered. And I can even feel them behind you now. I'm sure you feel very cold, don't you?' Afam stared at him with horror-filled eyes, too stunned to respond. Supervisor nodded, his expression, grave. 'It must have happened during your night shift yesterday after I'd gone. Tell me, did you leave the room at any time and re-entered without knocking?'

Afam nodded. 'NEPA took light and I went to look for a torch,' Afam's voice was as economical in volume as he was with the truth. He wasn't going to confess his cowardice to anyone.

'And when you found a torch, did you remember to knock three times when you returned?' Afam shook his head but Supervisor already knew the answer anyway. 'That's why I kept repeating the rules to you. But you young book people always think that you know better than your elders and betters. I bet you don't think I am a superstitious illiterate anymore, do you?' Afam looked away in shame. 'Oh yes, my boy. I know exactly what you think of me. I could read it in your eyes every time I spoke. Still, what's done is done. The issue now is how to resolve it.'

'I've already seen a doctor and he's sent me for some blood and urine tests.' Even as he spoke, Afam knew how ridiculous he sounded but he needed to have some control over what was happening to him. It had been a long time since he'd felt like a child or been spoken to like one, the way the supervisor was now addressing him.

'Doctor?' Supervisor barked a harsh laugh. 'My boy, no doctor on earth can cure you from what you've got. Take it from one who's had what you've now got.'

'You've had a follower?' Afam was stunned, but at the same time excited. For the first time since his life turned upside down, he was finally getting some answers that made sense. He felt sorry for all the times he had sneered at the supervisor and called him names behind his back.

'Of course I've had a follower. You can't work at the mortuary without getting a follower at one point or another, especially in your early days when you've still to understand how things operate.' Supervisor pulled up a chair and sat down, gesturing to Afam to do the same. 'But first things first. We have to identify who your follower is before we can move to the next step. Tell me, did you notice anything or hear anything unusual after you returned to the room last night?'

Afam began to shake his head then stopped. His brows furrowed as he tried to recollect a memory that was teasing the edges of his mind. *The strange sound...like scuttling mice... the strange swirling mist...and the girl, Ona... something not quite right about her arm and foot.*

Best to leave out the bit about the imagined presence breathing down his neck.

'I'm not sure if it's my imagination or not. But I think I heard something that sounded like mice scuttling towards that side of the room when I came back in,' Afam nodded towards the far right-hand corner of the morgue.

Supervisor nodded, as some wise elders in Afam's clan tended to do when thinking. 'Not your imagination, my boy. Anything else? Think, think.'

'Well, I think the girl…you know…Ona. I think her left arm was hanging down her side when I could have sworn they were folded together under her sheet earlier on. And her left foot was also exposed when I came in.' *There!* He'd said what had been niggling him all night but which he'd felt too embarrassed to discuss with anyone. *Till now.*

'Aha! Now we know!' There was a triumphant glint in Supervisor's eyes. 'I should have suspected it would be a woman. They tend to be the followers in the main, especially the young ones. They died before their time, you see, and they're not usually ready to go over to their ancestors yet. Also, they could have unfinished business, like the girl, who we know was murdered. I don't think the police have yet apprehended anyone for it, have they?'

Afam shook his head. He had been following the story intently since he first realised who the girl was. It was his opinion that the police would never find her killer. *But to have her as his follower....*Afam glanced towards the glass freezer where she had lain but which was now empty.

'She was taken today by her family for her funeral,' Supervisor said. 'I believe she will be buried tomorrow after the wake-keeping tonight. If that happens before you can shake her off, then I'm afraid you'll be stuck with her for your lifetime or till she decides to go, which may be never.'

Afam felt his heart begin to pound against his ribs. *A lifetime of this intolerable misery? A lifetime of having what was in effect a ghost, shadowing his every move? He would rather commit suicide.* Already, he felt an oppressive heaviness bearing down on his back, a chill that seeped right through to his marrow. He couldn't get himself to look at any of the other corpses in the room; such was his fear of yet another ghost following him about. He forced himself to resist the burning impulse to look behind him as he'd been doing all day.

Supervisor stood up, his movements decisive. 'Come; we have no time to lose. I'll call in a couple of warders to cover tonight's shift while we make our way to her village; Amankwo…in Eke town, I believe. I know the place. My cousin is married to a woman from that village.

It's not too far from the 9th Mile corner. We should be there in less than an hour if we leave now.'

Afam stared at the supervisor, his mouth agape. 'But... *Oga*, we can't just gate-crash her funeral,' he spluttered. 'I mean, what do we say to her people and what can we hope to achieve?'

'We hope to find her body and to send her back to her ancestors. Don't worry my boy. Trust me. We elderly people know how we go about these things. You're not the first neither will you be the last to be followed by a reluctant dead. But first, we have to go pick up some palm-wine, *Oji* kola nuts and a live rooster for our journey. Have you got any money?' Afam shook his head, embarrassed. 'No worries. You can pay me back when you get your salary next week.'

Supervisor called a number on his mobile and spoke for a few minutes. Then he picked up his hat and pulled out a bunch of keys from his trouser pocket. For the first time, Afam noticed a car key in the bunch. He'd never suspected the supervisor owned a car by the way he dressed. Mind you, with the amount of money he stole from the dead, he was probably rolling in it and just dressed down to avoid suspicion. Then Afam felt ashamed for his thoughts. The man was going to great lengths to help him and here he was harbouring uncharitable thoughts. He would buy

Supervisor a bottle of expensive Whiskey once this was over, whether or not they were successful in getting rid of his follower. This experience had shown him who his true friends were and that fat cow, Uzo, was certainly not on his list.

In no time, they were speeding down the express way in the supervisor's blue Peugeot, headed for the town of Eke, almost twenty-five kilometres away. The skies had darkened a deep grey/purple and traffic was sparse. In Supervisor's car boot, Afam could hear the big rooster throwing itself about as they sped along, gradually eating up the miles till finally, they arrived at the sandy roads of Eke in Udi Local Government Area, a town fabled for its beautiful women and scholarly men. It was a fact that the first Nigerian Judge at the World court, Justice Charles Dadi Onyeama, was from Eke. Afam wondered how they would be received by these intellectual villagers, especially when Supervisor explained their errand. He was already beginning to wish he hadn't come along on what he thought was a fool's mission. The people would laugh him out of their town; that was, if they didn't lynch them first for making a mockery of their grief. Yet, as much as he wanted no part of it all, the numbing chill that was now insidiously freezing up his limbs to icy chunks propelled him to follow the supervisor's lead. Add that to the terrible stench which had the supervisor winding down all his car windows, and he really had nothing to lose anymore.

There were cars parked everywhere when they finally arrived. Loud music and singing could be heard from several yards away as Supervisor finally manoeuvred his car into a tight spot between a lorry and a Peugeot saloon. Afam got out of the car and stretched, feeling his frozen limbs protest in agony. A full moon hung under the clear skies, swollen and bright. Everywhere was ablaze with lights from ad hoc electrical installations. Canopies and chairs where everywhere, with people milling about like an invasion of cockroaches. Afam could see women dancers, masquerade and acrobatic dancers, church choirs, disco jockeys and clans people dressed in uniform wrappers for easy identification. If one didn't know any better, one would think they had stumbled into a wedding celebration, rather than a funeral wake. But, Igbos are a race that celebrate deaths with the same respect and enthusiasm that births are celebrated. Each occasion is a celebration of the ancestors, welcoming them back to the clan or re-joining them for a new incarnation.

Supervisor made his way slowly towards the bungalow at the front of the compound, where Afam could now see important-looking men and women seated on plush sofas rather than the plastic chairs reserved for everyone else. He recognised the famous footballer, John Udo, amongst them - *the poor fiancé!* Afam had seen the man's haggard face in the newspapers as many times as he had seen Ona's own in the days following her disappearance. He felt sorry for him. It must be hard losing a loved one in such a brutal fashion, especially one as beautiful as Ona had been in her lifetime.

'Wait here,' Supervisor said, shouting to make himself heard above the din. Afam nodded. He was glad to stay where he was for as long as possible. Somehow, since they entered the compound of Ona's father, he had noticed a lessening of the chill and an ease at the back of his neck. When he mentioned it to Supervisor, he'd told him that Ona's ghost had simply taken a temporary leave to reconnect with her people and her home but that Afam shouldn't think she was gone for good. She would be back once she had meshed herself again with all that had been dear to her in life. At least, he was thankful that for the meantime, he could stand around the crowd without having people move away from him as if he were a resident of the leper colony at Oji River village.

Then it happened.

Just as he'd begun to relax and enjoy the uplifting song the choir were singing, he felt that familiar oppressive heaviness settle at his back and an icy chill pervade his entire body. People were sniffing, cursing aloud at everyone and no one, not yet sure who had fouled the air so vilely and shamelessly. But those closest to Afam were already feeling the unearthly chill and stench. They started moving away, at first slowly and then in a panic. Soon, people were pointing at him, cursing, scowling. Afam felt as exposed as Akalogholi, the naked lunatic that wandered the streets catching and eating flies. The area around him seemed suddenly desolate… cursed… like a place ravaged by a virulent plague. He wanted to hide, to be made invisible. He was a stranger in a strange place and never had his alien-ness hit him as strongly as then.

He saw a few young men headed his way, violence in their eyes and anger in their strides. His eyes searched wildly for Supervisor. *Should he run or stay? Where would he run to anyhow? He was in their village. He knew no one and they knew everyone. He would be as dead as their late clans-woman, Ona, in no time. No. Better he stood his ground. Surely, they wouldn't commit murder in front of the whole world. Most they could do was to manhandle him and chuck him out of the compound. He was fine with that. He wanted to be gone anyway.*

An uneasy silence descended amongst the crowd. All eyes were now glued on the young stranger dressed in abnormally warm clothing for that time of the year, standing alone, terror in his eyes. *Who is he? What's he done? Does anyone know him?* Afam sensed, rather than heard the questions on the crowd's lips, as the angry young men descended on him, grabbing his arms… only to let go with a shout!

'What? What?' People were asking, wondering why the men seemed unable to touch him, give him the beating he deserved. The young men backed away from him, just as the crowd had done minutes earlier, their hands covering their noses, an expression resembling fear and confusion in their eyes.

'That man's body is like ice block.'

'*Chei*! His skin almost burnt my hand when I touched him.'

'And the smell; it's like a rotten corpse.'

'That man is not alive, no way.'

'It's a ghost, *Onye Mmo*'

'Onye Mmo!'

'Onye Mmo!'

Afam heard the murmur grow, gathering in volume till it became a deafening roar. Then, a sudden melee of jostling, panicking bodies. People were screaming …shoving… desperate to get away from him. The atmosphere was charged with fear. Chairs tumbled to the ground; someone moaned. All was madness. Even the church choir abandoned their praise to God and joined the mindless flight. Afam saw John Udo, the footballer, escape into the open door of the bungalow, together with most of the dignitaries seated to the front of the compound.

'I'm not a ghost,' he shouted. 'I'm not a ghost.' But his voice was swallowed in the ruckus. Not that it would have made any difference anyway. Panic was an infection deaf to reason. Just then, Afam saw a man headed towards him, his arms outstretched. He was shouting something Afam couldn't hear. As he drew closer, Afam noticed that the man held a thick golden cross in his outreached hand and a bible in his other hand. *Dear Lord! A pastor from a Pentecostal church come to cast him out! That was all he needed.*

'You, son of Lucifer! Spawn of Beelzebub and Asmodius! In the Holy name of Our Lord Jesus Christ, conqueror of death, King of heaven and earth, I cast you back to the infernal hell from whence you've come! Go! In the name of Jesus Christ, lamb of God who taketh away the sins of this world, Go!' The Pastor pushed the cross and bible towards Afam's face, all the while keeping a healthy distance from him. Behind him, the remnants of his impressed choir members cheered and shouted "Amen", with the same gusto they had rendered their gospel songs just minutes earlier.

Afam couldn't help himself. He began to laugh. Soon, he was laughing so loudly tears streamed from his eyes. He knew he was edging close to hysteria, even madness. No sane person laughed like that at a funeral wake. Only a mad man or a demon. Was it little wonder they thought him one of Satan's minions! *Oh God! Holy Mary Mother of God! Please get me away from this madness. Where the hell was Supervisor?*

Just as Afam thought all was lost, he saw the supervisor walking towards him, accompanied by several men, mostly elderly men. Two of the men wore garbs Afam instantly recognised – *Dibias! God in heaven! Would this lunacy never come to an end? First, the wretched pastor and now, two witch-doctors. What next?* As they drew closer, one of the witch-doctors, the old one wearing three eagle feathers, let out a scream, pointing a gnarled finger at Afam.

'I see her! *Anu-Amankwo!* I see her!' The old man's eyes were filled with awe, tinged with terror. Afam glanced over his shoulders, feeling his skin crawl, breaking out in sudden goosebumps.

'I told you, didn't I? Now do you believe me?' Supervisor's voice was tinged in bitterness and triumph. He had not had an easy session with these elders. Unlike other elders he'd visited on similar errands in the course of his lifetime, these Eke Elders had been more sceptical than he'd ever experienced. *That's what came from dealing with a people that believed they were smarter than everyone else. Thank God their witch-doctors still remembered the old ways and knew their stuff. Now maybe they'd get on with the business at hand and send this poor girl back to her ancestors so he could return home for a good sleep before his day shift tomorrow.*

'Come, our son; follow us,' said the old man, taking Afam by the arm before promptly letting go with a startled cry. '*Chukwu! God!* Poor boy! Your burden is great indeed. Our daughter is strong on him.' Every one of the elders looked at Afam with compassion and suddenly, he felt his eyes fill up, un-maning himself before them. It had been a long time since anyone had shown him kindness. This had been the longest day of his life and he just wanted it over.

'We left the Rooster and Palm-wine in the boot of my car,' Supervisor said. 'One of you will have to accompany me to my car to get them.'

Afam was led into the bungalow by the rest of the elders while Supervisor and another elder went off for the items they'd brought along with them. Afam wasn't sure what they intended to do with the Rooster, *Oji* and palm-wine. But he was willing to go along with anything to rid himself of his unwanted follower. For some reason, he felt himself trusting the old witch-doctor with the eagle feathers. The man had seen something the others hadn't seen; something he himself couldn't see but felt as heavily as one laden with concrete.

They led him through the open door of the bungalow, towards the back of the house. Afam found himself in a room, empty, except for a table on which lay an open coffin. *Ona!* And once again, the wonderful bliss of release, freedom from the chill and pressure. He felt himself thawing, melting, sinking wearily to the bare floor, even as the elders rushed to hold him up, this time without difficulty.

'There she goes,' said the eagle-feathered witch-doctor, pointing towards the open casket housing Ona's beautifully made-up corpse. 'Our poor daughter! It will all be okay. Very soon, you will be with our fathers and mothers, those who will love you the best. And you will know eternal peace till you come back to us again, re-born and revenged.'

An old man in the room started to cry. The men went over to him and held his arm high up in the air.

'Agu! Great man! Father of strong sons! Unrivalled Farmer! Father of Ona, the most beautiful girl in the world! Hold your heart, our brother! Be a man! Soon it will be over! Ona will shortly be with our ancestors. *Ndo!* Sorry!

Our heart bleeds for you. Your pain is our pain, your loss, our loss.'

Afam stared at the man. *So that was Ona's father! Poor man!* Now that Afam looked closer, he could see that he wasn't as old as he'd first thought him. But grief had clearly aged him, giving him a headful of grey hairs atop a face still sporting some vestiges of youth. He wished he could do something to ease the man's pain. But he too was going through his own hell, through no fault of his; and all because of the man's dead daughter who wouldn't accept her death.

Just then, Supervisor stepped back into the room carrying the rooster. The other elder held the keg of palm-wine and *Oji* Kola nuts. To Afam's surprise, John Udo, the footballer, accompanied them in. His eyes were bloodshot and puffy, his expensive jacket rumpled and dusty. He looked like a man that seen the devil and all his minions. Afam felt a mixture of awe and pity. If the situation wasn't so dire, he would have asked the man for an autograph and taken pictures on his mobile to show his friends.

'Okay, let's begin. We haven't got much time. Lock the door and pull up a chair next to the coffin,' the second witch-doctor instructed. Someone rushed to obey. With a nod in Afam's direction, another elder guided him to the upright chair next to the open coffin. Afam sat down and averted his eyes. Even though he had washed that body and assisted in embalming it; even though for over a week, he had watched that body in its silent repose inside the drawer-freezer at the morgue; even though he knew every single feature in her face almost as well as he knew his own face… yet now, he just couldn't bear to look upon her corpse.

'Get the rooster and tie it to his ankle,' instructed the witch-doctor again. Afam looked in confusion at the supervisor. He felt helpless, with no control over his life or destiny. He had no idea what he was letting himself into. He'd never visited a witch-doctor in his life and had little faith in them. Seeing his bewilderment, the supervisor walked over to him and placed a hand on his shoulder.

'Don't worry, my boy,' he said. 'Very soon, everything will be over and we'll be back in our town in no time. Just trust these men and do whatever they tell you to do, okay? They are powerful men and know their art. Believe me, I have met many *Dibias* in my time and these two rank really high in my esteem.'

Afam nodded. He had no choice but to trust the men anyway. It wasn't as if he could do anything to halt the ceremony, even if he wanted to. Already, he could feel that familiar evil chill seeping through his skin, enveloping him in dread. He saw the eagled witch-doctor staring at him, the rheumy whites of his eyes protruding, his lips hanging.

'She is back with him again,' he murmured, nodding, shaking his *Ofo* sacred staff. John Udo looked as if he would faint, his wide eyes following the pointing finger of the witch-doctor. Afam felt the footballer's eyes on him and cringed in humiliation. This wasn't how he wanted to be seen by such a great man as John Udo; a village ignoramus tied to a live rooster, participating in pagan mumbo jumbo. His only consolation was that John Udo was also in it with him. His fate was tied to his own. They were all participants in this secret rite of exorcism, bound by the restless spirit of a murdered young woman.

'My son, listen carefully,' said the witch-doctor. 'I shall try and call our daughter back to her body. She will not want to leave you because she is afraid of her own body, which is cold and lifeless. They like to cling to life and anything living, just to get the heat of blood and the light of life. But she will go back to our ancestors, trust me. We will send her back tonight. But you must be brave. You will see and hear things that are strange to you. You will experience things outside your comprehension. But just know that you are inside this room with us. No matter where you find yourself, you are in fact, still in this room, okay?' Afam nodded, feeling more frightened than he'd ever been in his life. He was entering a dark and unknown realm. He would be alone, despite what the witch-doctor said. After all, he was the one with the follower, the reluctant dead, not them. *But God! He was so cold!* His teeth were rattling so hard he feared injury to his tongue. His entire body was shuddering like one experiencing an epileptic fit.

The witch-doctor poured a calabash of palm-wine on the floor of the room as libation to the ancestors. He called on *Anu-Amankwo*, the guardian god of Eke people, to come to their aid. With great deliberation, he began to break the Oji nuts and place the various segments on the dead girl's face.

As soon as he placed the first nut on her left eyelid, the bulb in the room began flickering furiously. All eyes glanced up nervously, then back again at the cold corpse in the casket. The witch-doctor turned to his eagle-feathered colleague.

'Where is she?' he asked.

'Still behind him. But she's not happy.'

'Tell her we want to help her; that her poor father wants her to be at peace.'

The eagled one repeated the message over Afam's head. Again, Afam felt his blood run cold. He now realised that this man was the one with the second sight, the only man that would communicate with the restless spirit hovering over him.

'She's looking very angry. I don't think she wants to go,' said the eagle-feathered one. Even as he spoke, Afam felt a heaviness pressing him forward in his chair, pushing… relentless… till his forehead almost touched his knees. He groaned in agony, trying to resist. But it was like fighting a hurricane. His limbs were too frozen to fight and his mind was getting fuzzy and confused. From a distance, he heard the witch-doctor intone some incantations…heard the other voices repeat a sonorous chant. A sudden shudder quaked his body, snapping his neck back just as the light bulb shattered to glassy fragments and the room went black.

And Afam ceased to exist...

******

He is walking along a dusty road, humming a little song underneath his breath. It isn't a happy song. He isn't really happy even though everyone expects him to be ecstatic. After all, his engagement could be announced today to a man everyone says is perfect for him. But he doesn't want to marry that man. He would rather remain a spinster than marry him, despite all his money and fame. He finds him arrogant and boastful, totally without class. He is also fake, always solicitous and respectful in front of his father but crass and loud once alone with him. Not that they've ever spent time alone away from his father's house. But the compound is large enough for them to walk about together, while the man spends his time on his mobile speaking to all kinds of people in a fake English accent he finds really irritating.

He has tried to tell his father how he feels but his father won't listen. Everyone thinks he's the right man with all his money and fame. But he prefers the young lawyer from Abia State, who is witty and gentle, despite not being as rich as the famous one. Well, today, he will finally make it clear to everyone that he intends to marry the lawyer. This is the twenty-first century after all and no one can force him to marry someone he doesn't love or even respect.

He's just about to flag down an Okada taxi when he hears a horn beep behind him. He turns round and recognises the big Mercedes car belonging to his unwanted suitor. Well, this is as good a time as any to break the news to him and tell him that marriage between them would be impossible because he has already promised himself to the lawyer from Abia State. He climbs into the car and smiles at the famous one. He tells him he is headed to Ogbete market to collect his birthday gown. The famous one asks again if he's still determined not to marry him despite knowing his father will be devastated with his decision. He says yes, his mind is made up. It's the lawyer for him.

Without warning, the famous one swerves his Merc and begins to drive in a different direction. He is alarmed and asks him what he's doing. The famous one turns a very ugly face at him.

'If I can't marry you then at least, I will enjoy your body,' he leers. He is laughing and driving so fast he starts to shake. He begins to plead with him to see sense, to take him back and he will do anything he says. But he continues laughing, loud and hard. It is an evil laugh that sends the chill of terror into his heart.

The famous one speeds along, his driving reckless. He seems to know exactly where he is going, as if he's planned his route beforehand. He tries to fight him, wrestle the steering from him, but he punches his face so hard he's almost blinded with pain. Now, his heart is really pounding. He feels a terror beyond anything he's ever felt. He will defend his honour to the very last. But what can he use against his superior strength? He's a sportsman after all, strong and athletic. All he has are his teeth and nails. But will they be enough?

He drives through a dusty, winding road and through a deserted farmland and stops the car. All around them are cassava plants atop mounds of dusty earth. He tries to open his door and run but the famous one catches him easily and throws him to the hard, dirty ground. He starts to tear off his dress and he tries to scratch him. He is screaming but no one hears him in the desolate farm.

He feels himself violated, the pain unbearable, the shame burning into his very soul. All he can think of is his poor lawyer who will now be getting a second hand bride - a soiled wife - defiled, ruined.

Just as he thinks it's all over, he feels his vile hands on his neck, gripping, choking the life from him. He starts to fight for his life. This time, all he can think of is poor Papa, who will never get a dowry after all.

Suddenly, a brilliant light blinds his vision, chasing away the drowning darkness of death. He looks at the light and his eyes widen with incredulity. Standing before him is Mama, beautiful, gentle Mama, who had joined the ancestors when he was yet to reach his teenage years!

But Mama is not alone. She is flanked by Grandmother Ada and Nne, Great-mother of the clan! Mama's face is sad but filled with love...dear Jesus! So much love that draws him to her. But Grandmother Ada and Great-mother Nne are not smiling. Their faces are like the dark clouds preceding a mid-day thunderstorm. They are bearing down on the famous one, murder in their eyes. He watches as they surround him, clawing at his cruel fingers round his neck, pulling, beating. He feels the sudden bliss of temporary release, as the famous one lets go briefly, his eyes flashing around like a startled thief.

'Leave your mark on him, our child! Rid him of his manhood that the world may know his shame!' Great-mother Nne shouts, her voice like a whisper in the wind. Yet, he hears it as if it is drummed into his ears by a thousand Adamma *masquerade drummers. But his hands are weak, his strength stolen by the terrible ordeal he's been subjected to by the vile apology to the human race still atop him.*

From the corner of his eyes, he sees a movement to his right, a flash of colours and a warming infusion of power, as the three women of his clan merge their souls with his and they become one; one bloodline, indivisible, inseparable, as it was always destined to be! And with the unity comes an incredible strength, an irresistible power from beyond the realms of mortals.

He reaches down and grabs the famed one's manhood and starts to pull, digging his nails into the soft flaccid skin with the combined strength and fury of the women that have loved him the best. He hears him scream in pain and shock, feels his hands squeeze even tighter round his neck, while another hand tries to wrestle his manhood from the ruining grip of his fingers. But he is fighting a force beyond the realms of humanity and he will not let go... they will not let go!

Even as the breath finally starts to seep from his lungs; even as he feels the eternal darkness descend on him, stealing him away from life into the warm embrace of his mother, he manages to cling on till he feels the soft flesh separate from its base, the famous one's agonised scream the last thing he hears as darkness finally descends.

And all is silent...

******

With a scream that pierced through the walls of the crowded room, Afam lunged from his chair and rushed to John Udo, pushing everyone aside with a superhuman strength that could not be challenged. In seconds, he had the powerful footballer on the floor, punching him, pummelling him, biting his hands, his ears, his face. He was screaming in a voice, discarnate, yet so high pitched it could only belong to a woman - a wronged woman - a very angry woman intent on vengeance. He felt hands trying to hold him back, pull him off the near-unconscious footballer. But they could not touch him. He was cloaked in ice and hate. With furious hands, he tore at the footballer's trousers, biting the man's hands as he tried to protect his nakedness.

'I ruined your manhood on the day you killed me. Today, the world shall see your shame,' he screeched in that uncanny female pitch that was as strange as it was familiar. He heard a collective gasp in the room as his words sank in, the furious scream of her father as the old man rushed towards the fallen hero and villain. Voices were shouting, cursing… and finally, he felt his anger abate, leaving him weak…drained… and suddenly, very, very sleepy.

'The rooster! The rooster! Untie the rooster now! It's caught her! It won't hold her for long. Quick!' He heard a voice he recognised as the eagle-feathered witch-doctor's issue the command. He felt the convulsed flaps of the voodoo chicken, frantic hands on his ankles, felt something whispery near his ears. He was sure he heard a small melodious voice whisper "thank you", but he couldn't be sure. Everything was fuzzy again. A warm blackness was stealing into his consciousness, a darkness without chills, without heaviness, without terrors.

Afam smiled and gave in to the dark……

A GOOD STUDENT

'...I only hear voices when those talking to me are dead.'
(James Herbert – Others)

My name is Ndu and I am a doctor. My wife and I would have a perfect marriage but for one bone of contention – our children's education. We were blessed with twin sons before her womb soured. Our boys are both healthy and boisterous but rather strong-willed. I admire their independent spirits even as I sometimes despair of their mischief. Nevertheless, I have insisted that they remain at home with us rather than adopt the general practice of sending children to the government boarding schools after their primary education. My wife on the other hand, having devoted over eleven years of our marriage rearing these two handfuls, is now desperate for a well-deserved break. She hopes to achieve this by sending them to a good boarding school like other boys their age.

But to this demand, I have resisted with the stubbornness of a Christmas ram being dragged to the butcher's knife. My wife says I am selfish. My sons say I am unreasonable and unfair. I stand in the way of all their freedoms and so they give me no peace in my own house. Only my mother understands; only my mother remembers the long years of terror that dogged me right through my teenage years till I finally graduated from University against my own expectations of myself. My wife thinks that my mother is an interfering old woman, intent on creating mischief in her son's marriage. But she knows nothing of the terrors that still haunt my sleep despite the passage of time and youth; terrors that have influenced every decision I have made in my life and marriage till date. So, my wife in her ignorance, constantly berates me and our otherwise happy marriage continues to be marred by this single bane.

******

I was sent to boarding school at the age of twelve years. Our protracted civil war with Nigeria had not long ended and things were still tough for our people. Even though the war ended with a declaration of "No victor, no vanquished", we Biafrans knew with every fibre in our starved bodies that we were the vanquished. The ruins of our bombed-out towns and the total desecration of our ancestral graves confirmed our vanquished status. Our town, Enugu, once the jewel of the federation, lay in ruins, her beauty battered, her people war-weary, victims of *kwashiokor* protein-deficiency and shell-shock.

Yet, within a few years of the end of hostilities, the indomitable spirit of our people raised our towns from the ashes of mortar destruction. Just like the fabled phoenix, our great towns of Enugu, Aba, Owerri and Onitsha were once more teaming with businesses, magnificent buildings and an impressive road network that brought in wealth and progress back to us again. Schools sprang up in almost every street and children exchanged war chants for nursery rhymes and hymns.

However, everyone knew that the Government secondary schools were the best boarding schools for children due to their superior resources. Competition for placements was stiff and usually ended in the hands of wealthy families or highly intelligent pupils. A few children like myself, who had lost their fathers to the civil war, were awarded placements because of *"Ima nmadu"*, having the right connections. My mother's sister was a teacher at one of those exclusive establishments and got me a placement in the school.

I arrived at St Saviours Government Secondary School, Enugu, having promised my tearful mother to write her a letter every week. With the exception of government offices, most people had no telephones in those early post-war years and communication was mainly through letters and mouth-to-mouth messages. It was on my first day at school that I met John Nwandu. We were both in Lord Lugard house. As was the practice in early post-colonial Nigeria, most places, from streets to schools, were named after some colonial leader or pioneer. Our school house was named after the first governor-general of Nigeria, Lord Frederick Lugard, whom I later learnt viewed us as nothing better than "attractive animals" and indolent liars.

I noticed John Nwandu on his arrival, as he stood out from the rest of the boys on account of his gold-rimmed glasses. Reading glasses were a great luxury in those days and I figured John's parents must be wealthy even though he displayed none of the arrogance and brashness of the other boys from rich homes. John was shy and studious. He was rather frail in health and I soon discovered that he was a sickler, one of those unfortunate kids that had the dreaded sickle-cell anaemia disease.

John and I hit it off from the start despite our differences. While John was small and weak, I was big and burly. While he was naturally brilliant, I plodded along as best I could to get average grades. Although John couldn't play the boisterous games of football and basket-ball, he played a mean game of scrabble.

In our first term at school, John suffered bouts of his sickle-cell "crisis" as he called the mind-numbing pain that tortured his shivering body at regular intervals. At such times, it fell on me to administer his painkillers, massage vapour rub on his swollen joints and force hot liquids down his resisting throat. I lived in fear of John dying from one of his attacks but he assured me that people tended to grow out of the sickness in time. He planned to be a doctor when he grew up, he said, curing people like himself.

John's parents lived in a different city quite a distance from our school. But they visited him frequently, bringing all kinds of delicacies for him, even apples all the way from England. They included me in their generosity, since for some reason they viewed me as John's saviour at St Saviours. On numerous occasions following John's sickle cell crisis, I would ask him to return to his city and attend a day school near his home. But John was always adamant in his refusal. He would not let his sickness dictate his life. Boarding school was good for him, he said. He was free of his mother's constant molly-coddling and learning to deal with his crisis on his own. Anyway, it was just a matter of time before he outgrew the disease.

John fought his illness right through our first grade with quiet fortitude. But in our second year, his crisis seemed to get worse rather than better. On a few occasions, his parents had to collet him from school for hospitalization at the city's general hospital. But he always came back bright and cheerful, determined as ever to be the good student he was. He would work extra hard to catch up on missed lessons and still found time to assist other classmates with homework. Little wonder he was loved by all. His illness gave him a maturity beyond his years and he took everything and everyone in his calm stride. Even the school bullies ended up being more protective of him than his fussy mother. John had that effect on people. The teachers loved him although he did nothing to be a teacher's pet. He neither carried tales nor sucked up to the prefects. He was just himself, a shy, gentle and wise little old man in the body of a thirteen-year old boy.

*****

That summer, I got an invitation from John's parents to spend part of the long vacation with them. And soon, I found myself in their big Mercedes car, cruising the potholed asphalt to that famed city of Onitsha, with its famous market and equally famous river, the River Niger. It was also a historical town, the home of Dr Nnamdi Azikiwe, Nigeria's first president. I can honestly say that I had never experienced such luxury as I enjoyed in John's house that unforgettable summer of our thirteenth year. Their house had eight rooms with three reception rooms. There were at least four cars parked outside their large compound, all belonging to John's parents. We had a chauffeur-driven car to ourselves which took us all around the old city of Onitsha and surrounding towns. John and I played together, ate together and grew as close as twin brothers with none of the rivalry at times associated with that relationship.

But like all good things, the utopian experience came to an end…rather too soon for me. I was sorry to leave John's home but knew we would meet up at St Saviours in less than two weeks when the new term resumed. The rest of the holiday was a blur, as all I thought of was returning to boarding school and showing off my new acquisitions.

On my return to school, the first person I met up with was John - of course. We shoved each other happily and exchanged a few pleasantries before I noticed that John seemed different. It took me a few minutes to realise that he wasn't wearing his glasses. His eyes sparkled with the brilliance of a thousand bulbs and he was more animated than I had ever known him to be, laughing heartily, his voice loud, arms gesticulating and legs as restless as ants.

'Never felt better in my life,' John laughed, giving my arm a friendly bash when I voiced my surprise at the dramatic change in both his looks and his personality. 'It's just great being back at school again.' My face creased in a wry smile. *Typical.* While most of us prayed for lessons to be deferred indefinitely, the Johns of this world couldn't wait to wallow in school work like pigs in mud.

Between the two of us, we unpacked my brand new suitcase, courtesy of John's parents. I ensured my new acquisitions were displayed in prominent positions around our double bunk where other students couldn't help but notice and hopefully grind their teeth in envy. I gave little thought to the fact that most of the students were from affluent homes anyway and probably had better stuff than I. In all the excitement, it took me time to realise that John hadn't unpacked his suitcase; that in fact, he had no suitcase to unpack.

'I forgot it in the boot of our car,' John said when I asked. 'Hopefully, our driver will find it later and bring it back to me. In the meantime, I'll just have to share your stuff if it's okay with you?' John made it a question rather than a statement, polite and considerate as ever despite knowing everything I had was more or less paid for by his parents.

Soon, we were all settled, catching up with the other students and talking about the girls we'd met, fancied and conquered over the long summer holidays. The dinner bell interrupted our reckless lies and to everyone's amazement, John announced that he was starving and could eat a whole ram. We all burst into laughter. A starving John was a first in our dictionary.

'Sure, Birdie,' I mocked. 'Let's go stuff you up with seeds.' We all laughed as we headed to the large communal refectory. But we were in for a shock. John gobbled up everything in sight. He shoved down the food as if *Tiv warrior*s were at his heels, armed with bloodied machetes. Soon, a lively discussion broke out in the surrounding tables. More and more extras were passed to John by the amused kids, eager to see how long his gluttony would last. To our consternation, he ate up everything in sight. It was as if his stomach had suddenly become a bottomless pit.

Over the following weeks, John continued to eat like a *Calabar* bride in a pre-wedding fattening house. Yet, he never put on an ounce of fat to his slender frame. Even more conspicuously, his sickle cell crisis disappeared as if cured by a *Dibia*'s powerful juju. It seemed he had at last grown out of it as he'd predicted, which probably accounted for his ravenous appetite - making up for lost time…or lost food, as I teased. John's parents hadn't visited him since the beginning of term and I put it down to his recovery from that deadly sickness. In every way, John was the proverbial picture of health. That brilliance I'd noticed in his eyes on our first day at school never diminished in its intensity. If anything, his eyes burnt more iridescently as the weeks flew.

John went on to develop a cat's vision, seeing so clearly in the dark that students began to call him by the nick-name, *Usu,* bat. One particular incident stood out in my mind. It happened on our way back from evening prep. It was not unusual for students to come across the occasional snake or scorpion in both the dormitories and the vast grounds of the school. Most of us carried either torches or kerosene lamps to light up our paths after evening prep. On that particular night, our torch batteries had died out on us but snakes and scorpions were the last things on our minds as we made our leisurely way back to Lord Lugard House.

So, my shock knew no bounds when John suddenly pulled me back with a hard yank on my arm and stooped to pick up a wriggling black piece of venom with his bare hands. *Echieteka!* The infamous deadly viper whose victims rarely survived to the next sunrise, hence its name, *Echieteka - tomorrow is too long to live.*

I watched with a mixture of horror and awe as John coolly squeezed the life out of that deadly viper and flung it away into the nearby bush as if it was nothing more than orange pulp. John seemed to think nothing of his extraordinary action, pulling me along by my unresisting arm as if everything was normal.

'Johnnie, how in God's name did you see *Echieteka* in the dark?' I held him back by the arm. 'I mean, how come it didn't bite you? This is crazy… I mean, no one will believe me when I tell them what I saw tonight.'

'Well, don't tell them then,' John shrugged. 'It's no big deal…honest.'

'Huh! No big deal, he says. Maybe not to you, my friend. But it's a mega deal to me. Shit! You saved my life, Johnnie. Without you, I'd probably be dead by tomorrow morning and my father's name would be lost forever.' I tried to make light of the matter to hide my emotions, feelings which alternated between immense gratitude and confusion, awe and something close to fear. *How did he see that black viper in the pitch dark?* The question played in my mind all through that night and many more nights after that incident.

I noticed that other students were soon seeking out John to help them find missing articles. Somehow the story had gone round the school that John could find any lost item, be it stolen or plain missing. He would calmly pick up a bible hidden under a pillow and withdraw some stolen money or pull out a set of missing keys from the pocket of a freshly laundered pair of shorts. John never seemed to find anything peculiar about his uncanny ability to recover stuff and as the weeks passed, his popularity grew to such an extent that he was constantly surrounded by new friends. His new popularity would have made me jealous had I not known I was still his number one best friend. Still, his sudden fame continued to amaze me as John hadn't been one to socialise in the past due to his illness and studious nature.

I watched in amazement as he proceeded to join almost every club in the school, from debating club to drama club, tennis club to the school choir. And in every single activity, he excelled. From a frail weakling who could only manage to walk to classes on a good day, John metamorphosed into a football pro and a long-jump champion, jumping distances never before witnessed in the school's history. The teachers couldn't sing his praises enough, especially as he still continued to excel in class tests.

Then something strange happened. Our form teacher, Mrs Ukah, whose duty it was to ensure that her class was up to date with their school fees, walked into our class one morning and began calling out the names of those owing fees. The names held no surprises for us since we already knew the handful of students from poor families who were inevitably late with their fees. I would have been amongst them but for the generosity of my aunt who was a teacher at St Saviours.

As Mrs Ukah reeled out the names of the debtors, the rest of us who were up to date with our fees eyed the humiliated students smugly, as if it was by our own efforts that our fees were paid. Then the bombshell fell. John's name was called out as one of the students in the red and the entire class gasped, turning to stare at him in stunned disbelief.

Everyone knew that John's parents were truly minted. They made generous donations to the school on inter-house sports days and John was always the first to pay his fees. It was therefore impossible for John's name to be on the same shameful page as the rest of the peasants in our class.

One student raised his hands to remind Mrs Ukah that she had mistakenly called out John Nwandu's name. Our teacher assured John that he in fact owed his school fees. But she was quite gentle with him, telling him not to worry himself unnecessarily since it was surely an oversight by his busy parents. She was sure it would be rectified in no time. John explained that his parents had planned to travel to New York, U.S.A, on holidays. *Auh! That explained things.* The teacher was more interested in the habitual debtors, the students from wretched backgrounds who had to be harassed and threatened with expulsion before their parents found their fees by begging or stealing.

'You never told me your parents had travelled to America,' I said to John later that afternoon, my voice accusing. I wasn't happy that he was keeping secrets from me just because he now had other friends. After all, I was the only one in school that had ever stayed at his parent's posh home in Onitsha.

'Slipped my mind,' John replied, his tone casual. 'I'm not sure if they've travelled yet. All I know is that there was talk of a holiday in New York just before I left home.'

I thought he was lying, though I couldn't figure out why he would lie about his parent's whereabouts. Probably embarrassed about owing fees for the first time and made up the story to cover his shame. On the other hand, he might be telling the truth. After all, his suitcase was yet to arrive, something I didn't think would be the case were his parents in the country. So, I let it go and we continued with our normal routine of daily academic drudgery, until that fateful day the head-teacher summoned John to her office, a day that shattered my life and abruptly ended my time at St Saviours Government Secondary School, Enugu.

What I'm about to relate now may sound fantastical, even insane. But I assure you it did happen. Just as day follows night and the rain falls from the skies, what I witnessed on that terrible day is as real as the fingers on my two hands. Twenty seven years on, and it is still as fresh in my mind today as if it happened yesterday. How can I forget even a single detail from that day when it literally changed my entire life and beliefs?

It happened this way.

*****

We had just finished having our literature lesson. It was a hot day as I recall, just about lunch-time. The sun was fierce in the skies, burning through the asbestos roofing of our classroom and leaving us sweat-soaked in that stuffy paper-littered room. Yet, we were happy - mischief-laden - making fun of our literature teacher's proclivity to exaggeration, our voices female-pitched in mimicry.

It was in the middle of this rowdy interlude that a boy from the junior classes peered through one of the open windows of our classroom and asked if anyone was called John Nwandu. His voice was hesitant, his face wearing a timid look...as rightly it should. Junior boys had no business in the terrain of their seniors and betters.

'Who wants to know, mite?' growled a classmate, struggling to suppress his mirth at the terrified look on the lad's face.

'Sir, Mrs Eze said to tell him to come to her office at once,' the boy's voice was almost a whisper.

'Hey, John!' called out our classmate. 'This rat here says the Head wants you in her office, pronto. What's up?'

'Dunno,' John shrugged. 'Hey mate, accompany me, would you? We'll grab ourselves a moi-moi *bean cake afterwards. What d'you say?'*

John didn't need to ask me twice, moi-moi *or no* moi-moi. *I was curious to know why the Head wanted him. It was a rare thing for the rather aloof Head to request the presence of any student unless they were getting expelled or suspended. I couldn't imagine John at the risk of either punishment. John didn't seem fazed by the message; neither was I. After all, he was a good student, a model student. He could only be wanted for something positive.*

On getting to the office, the Head's secretary, a nasty spinster who loathed the students as much as we detested her, gave John a peculiar look and without preamble, ushered him straight into the Head's office.

'Not you,' she barked at me as I made to follow John. Her face held a sour look that implied I was a very nasty thing in her sight. I shrugged and made to sit on one of the chairs in her office. But she gave me such an evil look I thought better of the idea and instead, slouched

across to the farthest corner of the office and leaned against the wall, feigning cool disinterest, my hands in my trouser pockets. There were a couple of visitors waiting their turn to see the Head in the secretary's office, a crippled man with walking sticks and a fat woman, no doubt some boy's parents. I adjusted my tie and arched my brows. It was vital that I showed them how cool I was, how well I fitted into the exclusive fraternity of the almighty St Saviours. Dear heavens! The silly vanities of youth!

John had barely opened the door to the Head's office when I heard a piercing scream shatter the relative quiet of the office. The screams went on and on as I dashed into the Head's office before the secretary could get her mammoth backside out of her chair. Behind me I heard the sudden pandemonium as people crowded the office eager to find the source of the screams. But I had no interest in them. All that mattered to me was that my friend John was trapped inside that room with whoever was emitting those spine-chilling shrieks.

What I witnessed in the Head's office that terrible October's afternoon will remain in my memory till my dying day. The first person I saw was John's mother, Mrs Nwandu, that gentle sophisticated lady that had treated me to the most wonderful summer vacation of my life. Except that the woman before me was a mockery of the lady I had so admired. She was dressed in ill-fitted lace wrapper, her Enigogoro *high scarf askew on her head. Her back was pressed against the farthest wall of the Head's office, her bandaged arms covering her face as she screamed and screamed. Her eyes, terror-wide, were glued on her only son in utter horror. I noticed our class teacher, Mrs Ukah, cowering with the Head behind her large rectangular desk laden with files and books. Their eyes were as terror-filled as John's mother's and small whimpering sounds emitted from their slack mouths.*

And John... my poor friend, John. He stood in the centre of the room as one lost, his features cloaked in bewilderment and tears, pleading to a mother too terror-stricken to give him any solace or love.

'Mama! Please...it's me John...your son,' he cried, stretching out his arms to his mother. But she clamped her lids, shutting him out of her sight, even as her mouth continued to emit those blood-curdling screams. I rushed towards John and made to grab his arm. But the arm I touched that day in the Head's office was a frozen log. It was the arm of a corpse. I could see an icy mist slowly building around my friend, even as I heard the Head scream out, 'Don't touch him! He's a ghost! He's dead! Oh God! Help us! A ghost...a ghost...' The women were

gibberish, all dignity and authority gone. John's mother was still screaming, her voice getting hoarser and weaker.

But the word, "ghost", had already taken root in the senses of the crowd gathered outside the Head's office. I heard the melee around me, as students and teachers alike stampeded out of the room screaming, "Onye Mmo!" "ghost!" *The Head and our class teacher bolted from the room with the rest of the crowd, leaving me alone with a terrified mother whose screaming was fast rendering unconscious and a solitary boy, forlorn and frightened. Confusion was written on every feature of John's face.*

John turned to me, his arm outstretched and I, in my mortal cowardice and eternal shame, backed away from him, shaking my head, rejection and horror in my every stance.

'Tom…Tom, please say I'm not a ghost,' John pleaded, tears forming rivulets on the planes of his face. I shook my head weakly, inching away from him in terror. Yes; my name then was Thomas and just as the biblical Thomas doubted and denied our Lord's resurrection, I denied my best friend and brother, John Nwandu, in the hour of his greatest need.

Even now…Dear Jesus! Even now, I still see the pain in his tragic eyes as he looked at me, a look filled with immense sadness and sorrow. The burning brilliance in his eyes slowly diminished and I could no longer hold his gaze. I saw the slumped figure of John's mother by the wall and suddenly, everything felt surreal. I felt disconnected from myself, as if I was watching "Randall and Hopkirk" *on the big television in John's posh house all over again, only this time in horrible slow motion.*

'I'm not a ghost... I'm not a ghost,' I heard John's whispered insistence; saw him shaking his head in negation of a truth I was beginning to behold. I could hear the students chanting outside the staffroom, "Onye Mmo... *John Nwandu is a ghost!" Their voices were frenzied, piercing. And the louder they screamed, the more unsubstantial John became.*

Right in front of my stunned gaze, I saw him begin to dissolve. Bit by slow bit, his body started to disintegrate like fluffy flakes of white cotton. Somehow, he was no longer clothed and a brilliant light of dazzling whiteness shrouded his disappearing form. I saw him change from a solid figure to a translucence presence that was as terrifying as it was incredible to witness. An awful tremor shook his fast vaporizing form, causing a matching reverberation in the room. The temperature in the office suddenly dropped to sub-zero in the middle of the sweltering African noonday.

Then...things began to fly. Like a place hit by a sudden hurricane, files flew from the Head's table, books tumbled to the floor, chairs skated across the room and the overhead bulb shattered to a million pieces, causing me to duck between the heavy book shelves by the door of the office. My hands clenched over the wooden edges of the shelves as I struggled to hold onto my sanity in that room of horror. I saw the books tumble around me from the shelves, narrowly missing my head. And in the mist of the fear, I kept hearing that pitiful yet persistent voice pleading his humanity... his existentiality... his voice getting hoarser...fainter...before fading into the icy chill of the Head's Office.

The last thing I heard that formless voice whisper was, 'Mama, I'm not a ghost. Mama....Mama...'

Then silence...

...a total absence of sound, as terrifying as the violent fury of a few seconds before. Even the students' ruckus outside the room froze momentarily, as if a ghost or an angel from God had walked into their midst. A terrible chill suddenly descended on me and I did something I had never done before that day or after.

I fainted.

One second I was cowering between the heavy oak book shelves, my teeth rattling with cold and terror, my feet quaking in the leather Cortina shoes John's parents had given me that beautiful summer holidays so long ago now, its innocence stolen by the corruption of untimely death. Then the next second, I was flat out on the worn brown carpet in the Head's office, the sanity-deserted screams of John's mother still ringing in my head, before she too became mercifully silent.

*****

I have little recollection of what transpired over the next few weeks as I was in a state of shock. They said I was incoherent, talking gibberish, my body wracked with tremors like an epileptic. I remember nothing of that day from the time I lost my sanity and consciousness in the doomed office of the headmistress. The Head ordered my transfer to the general hospital and then to my mother's house. That day was the last I saw of my school, the great St Saviours, whose grounds I once proudly strode with my friend and brother, John Nwandu.

From that terrible day, I became a victim of incurable fears, which made it impossible for me to attend any school. I struggled to come to terms with the fact that the dead did not stay buried; that they could return to the living anytime and anywhere; that everyone you came across could well be a walking dead. I was fighting for my sanity, struggling with the terrible nightmares that had become my lot since that fateful day in the head's office; nightmares of a spectral John, decayed flesh dropping in putrid clumps off the grinning mask of his skull, begging …pleading with me to accept him as human - as my friend. His hand on my skin was always cold…clammy…dead. I would wake up drenched in my own sweat, praying for death, for release, his voice still ringing hollow in my ears.

Worst of all was the guilt, the crippling soul-killing guilt at my rejection of my beloved friend in his hour of need; the knowledge that my betrayal contributed to his final dissolution. My mind was tortured day and night by the shameful fact that I had been tested and found wanting by the one true friend I ever had. I was consumed by the guilty knowledge that I hadn't loved John as well as I should have done. My name, Thomas, was a cursed name, the name of a traitor. Never again would I be burdened with that name of treachery.

Through it all, through all my troubles, my mother tended to me, patient as Christ Himself. She listened to my insane ramblings and offered me warm comfort as only a mother could. She kept me at home till I was brave enough to attend a day school near our house. Still, the terrors haunted me in my new school. I was convinced every student was a potential ghost and that every ghost would seek me out like flies to a putrid carcass. I made no friends and kept my own counsel. *Safer that way.* My school work suffered and for a while I considered quitting education for good.

But one thing kept me going, one glimmer of light and hope - the memory of my late friend, John Nwandu. John had been a good student. He had tried his best to make me a good student in his short lifetime. He was going to be a great doctor one day before death's cruel claws snatched him from life before his time. Ironically, it wasn't the sickle cell anaemia that had killed him in the end; a freak car accident on his way back to school after our glorious summer vacation. John had died instantaneously while his parents had survived with serious injuries. His father went into a coma but his mother recovered to bury her only child and mourn the loss of a truly good son.

Then the strange letter from the school, requesting John's school fees in full to avoid suspending him from classes. His mother had only come to officially inform the school of her son's death as well as to castigate them for not showing any concern about the prolonged absence of her son from school. Only to find that her dead son had continued his fatally interrupted journey to St Saviours, to complete what he had set off to do - take his classes, pass his exams and become a doctor.

As I said, John was a good student and good students do not quit school, not even for the mighty will of death. Through the years, I mourned my friend and brother, John Nwandu, with every fibre in my wretched body and swore to his memory that I would complete my schooling…for him; only for his sake. I would become the doctor he never got to be and help sickle cell sufferers lead as painless a life as I could give them. My life would be a celebration of life not death - and most definitely, not treachery.

My name is now *Ndu,* meaning "life" and I am a doctor. My wife is a good woman and our twin sons are good students. But they are day students, attending a nearby secondary school in our town. I refuse to allow them to live in a boarding school, not even for the sake of a peaceful marriage. I will not be John Nwandu's mother, should heaven forbid, I lose any of my sons to death's greedy jaws. I shall not stumble across the ghosts of my sons because they live in a boarding school where anonymity is preserved and the dead roam without fear of exposure. As I said, my sons are good students and they live with me.

HADIZA

'...My God, I felt her. I can smell her. It feels like she went through my soul!'

(James Khan – Poltergeist)

Khalid's decision to divorce his wife, Hadiza, had not been an easy one. But then, nothing in his life had been easy. Growing up fatherless, uneducated and destitute had not been easy. His decision to abandon the Christian religion of his Igbo tribe for Islam had not been easy either. It had taken him a long time to get people to address him by his new Islam name, Khalid, same with his wife, Hadiza, whose original name had been *Ngozi,* (God's blessing) a decent and worthy Igbo name. In fact, some relatives still persisted in calling him Daniel, his original Christian name, out of sheer bloody-mindedness and spite. The head of his clan, his uncle Ezekiel, had threatened to excommunicate him from the clan for the disgrace. No self-respecting Igbo man would stain his ancestor's honour by taking on the accursed religion of the savage Hausa tribes, the same people that had massacred the Igbos in the bloody civil war which had taken the life of Khalid's father, amongst other worthy sons of Biafra.

But Khalid was not nick-named "*Okwute*" (rock) just for his stocky build. He was as hard as stone where his needs were concerned and being rich was one of his greatest needs. Becoming a Moslem had been a financial investment rather than a spiritual enlightenment. It opened the gateway to the wealthy Moslem fraternity of the North, enabling him to trade in cattle and foodstuff before his eventual initiation into the highly lucrative fuel distribution cartel. He was now a man of respect despite his illiteracy. He had an honorary doctorate degree from one of the universities in the country, thanks to his generous donations. He could now legitimately prefix his name with the prestigious title of "Dr", just like the arrogant intellectuals that looked down their noses at him because of his uneducated status. These days, he called the tune in the clan despite his uncle's role as clan leader.

It was therefore of little concern to him that his uncle and the extended family disapproved of his decision to divorce Hadiza, his wife of nine years, in order to marry his mistress, Latoya, an African-American divorcee he'd met on one of his frequent trips to the United States. Khalid had watched his wife go from a slender, docile and beautiful young bride to an obese and obedient mother of three. She had yielded to his insistence that she become a Moslem wife despite her strong Christian upbringing. She took up the Koran and covered herself with the dark and unattractive hijab which he knew she detested, just to please him.

But while she was a good mother and wife, anticipating and catering to his every need, Khalid no longer desired Hadiza as a woman. He knew his inability to make love to her was a source of great unhappiness to her though she tried to mask it with that gentle smile she reserved especially for him. Hadiza was aware of his infidelities; he never hid them from her. But as a good Moslem wife, she accepted them, subservient to his needs as was her duty under the teachings of the Koran. He made sure he kept her and their three sons in comfort and that was more than most other husbands did. Her forbearance however, began to make him feel guilty and the guilt soon bred a resentment that culminated in his decision to take a second wife.

His intended bride, Latoya, was a liberated woman of the West; sophisticated, witty, sensual and most importantly, educated. She was like no other woman he'd ever known. She respected nothing and nobody. Her very indifference was like an aphrodisiac to him. She lived hard, worked little and played hard. Although she was only two years his senior, she already had two divorces under her belt. He would be her third and hopefully, last husband. He was still in shock that such a woman would consent to be his wife, an American no less!

Everything was going according to plan except for one hitch - Latoya wanted Hadiza out of his life for good. Khalid had agreed to a registry marriage as demanded by Latoya, despite his preference for a Moslem ceremony. He had even promised to send Hadiza and her children away, even as Abraham cast away the faithful concubine Hagar and her son into the desert. He went further to promise Latoya a separate and more luxurious home for both of them, provided she agreed to let Hadiza retain her title of first wife.

But Latoya had no intentions of being anybody's second wife. She belonged to a Western civilization that recognised one wife and one hundred percent monogamy. There was no space in her life for a spare wife, first or otherwise. Hadiza had to be divorced or no marriage - all or nothing, period.

For months, Khalid wrestled with his conscience or what was left of it, trying to come up with a solution to his dilemma. He felt bad about what he intended doing to Hadiza and did not relish the prospect of adding a humiliating divorce to her list of indignities. Knowing his wife, he knew she would go quietly when the chips were down, without much fuss, like the good Moslem wife she was. That was part of the problem with their marriage, Hadiza's total lack of spunk and adventure. Perhaps, if she had devoted less time on the kids and more time on him, then Latoya wouldn't have been an issue in their lives. In the end, Hadiza had really been the architect of her own doom. He refused to be held to ransom by pity.

Khalid called Hadiza into his bedroom just as she was about to retire for the night and told her he would be divorcing her. She stared at him numbly, her eyes pain-filled, unable to take in the enormity of his words. Then she fell to her knees before him, clasping his resisting hands, her movements feverish, desperate.

'Khalid, husband of my heart, father of my sons, what have I done to deserve this wrong?' She wailed, tears pouring unheeded down the smooth planes of her plump face. 'Have I not given you sons and secured your lineage? Have I not been a chaste and obedient wife to you? Have you forgotten your promise to me when you begged me to marry you, that you would cherish me for eternity? Why do you bring this shame on me now? Don't you love me anymore?'

Khalid looked away, unable to hold her gaze or stem the flood of emotions her words raised in him. Once…a long time ago…Hadiza had been the most beautiful woman he'd ever seen. He had felt honoured and blessed to be her husband. Regret stirred briefly in his heart but then, he looked into the fat, tear-streaked face of his wife and Latoya's sultry image superimposed itself in his mind's eye. His vision became clouded. He ceased to see the good woman beyond the outer folds of flesh. With a violent shove, he pushed Hadiza away from him and strode to the door. He paused, looking at the crumbled form on the plush flooring of his bedroom, his eyes cold, his face remote. Then, in line with the Sunni divorce procedure, he uttered the *Talaq* three times in succession - *I divorce you, I divorce you, I divorce you.*

And it was done. Khalid was a free man. He had not even given Hadiza the three months grace prescribed by Islam between each pronunciation of the *Talaq*. He simply severed her from his life as if she was no more than over-ripe fruit from a second-rate market stall.

His relatives thought he had lost his mind. *Who in their right mind would divorce such a good woman who had sacrificed so much for his sake?* They were even more horrified that he planned to marry a foreigner, a woman not even from the shores of Nigeria, who was both his superior in age and divorce tally.

His uncle Ezekiel, against his better judgement, eventually accepted custody of Khalid's three sons. Latoya wanted no part of them in her matrimonial home and to let Hadiza keep them was out of the question. It would be an abomination to reject the sons of the clan and Khalid had promised to provide generously for his children's upkeep. Hadiza was sent back to her people, two villages away, and Khalid severed all contact with her.

As promised, he set up the luxury home Latoya demanded and in no time, she was throwing lavish parties for her fellow expatriates, drinking, smoking and dancing till day-break every weekend. Khalid felt an outsider at these parties, which he came to resent and dread as one dreads greedy in-laws. Worse, Latoya showed no signs of embracing Islam as she'd promised she would once he divorced his wife. Her infidel and amoral lifestyle was beginning to affect his standing amongst his Moslem business associates.

Things were no better at the home front either, where his sons presented sullen and resentful faces to him whenever he visited them. He couldn't blame them for their attitude but there was little he could do to remedy the situation save to divorce Latoya, which was something he would never do. She was a fever in his blood…an addiction…too intoxicating to let go. He was providing his kids and his uncle with more luxuries than they'd ever dreamed possible. *What else did they want from him…his blood?*

*****

In a small airless room, overflowing with clothes and boxes, Hadiza lay on a single metal bed, staring up at the sluggish rotations of the overhead ceiling fan. Her henna-patterned hand lay languidly on her brow. Her eyes were wide, overly bright with a feverish glint coating her pupils. Her body was so still that she appeared unconscious, save for the intermittent blinks of her long-lashed lids and the rapid rising of her chest underneath her flower-print night dress. Though the short needle on the square wall-clock pointed to three o'clock in the afternoon, Hadiza had yet to stir from her bed. Its rumpled sheets and discarded pillows were a testament to the sleepless nights and restless days she'd endured since her ignominious expulsion from her marital home eleven months gone. *Why? Why? What had she done to deserve this shameful fate, stuck in a spare room in her father's house, a charity-case with little respect, when once she'd been the favoured daughter, wife of a wealthy husband who lavished her family with luxuries of every kind? Hadn't she sacrificed everything for her marriage, just to make Khalid happy and keep her marriage and family together? She would have turned a blind eye to his affair with the American harlot as she had done with all his other indiscretions. She knew they meant nothing to him, just a man relieving himself of his semen overload as Khalid had explained to her the first time it happened when she was pregnant with their first son. She was the one he loved, the one he had married, the only one he would cherish for eternity. So why had he broken his promise, turning her into an object of pity for all? How was it possible that he could forget her so completely as if she'd never existed? She, who had borne him three fine sons, loved him with every breath in her lungs, given nine years of her life in selfless servitude to him. He didn't have to divorce her. Most men married three, four...even, six wives. She would have stayed on as his first wife without a fuss.*

With a sudden jerk, Hadiza leapt from her bed and began pacing around the tiny room, her movements terse, manic, like a caged hyena. She kept wringing her hands with the frenzy of Macbeth's wife, like one washing out a bloodied hand, her breathing short and harsh in the tight confines of the room. From a distance, she heard a tentative knock on her door, heard the knob turn, felt curious eyes boring into her turned back. *What did they want? To laugh at her, witness her shame all over again? Why won't they leave her alone with her misery? Why wouldn't Khalid answer her questions? "Don't you love me anymore?" she'd asked him. Surely, that was an easy enough question to answer. A simple "Yes" or "no" was all it would take. It wouldn't have killed him to tell her if he felt anything for her...no matter how small...after all their years together.*

Or had it all been a farce? Had their entire time together been one big lie? How could a man go from loving a woman so desperately one minute to rejecting her so completely without just cause in a blink of an eye?

Behind her, Hadiza heard the door shut gently, heard a worried female voice, her mother, speak in hushed tones, 'She's at it again, pacing about and lost in her thoughts. She hasn't touched her plate in days. Maybe we should consider calling in the mad-people's doctor. Just that it would be such a shame on our family name…on top of everything else. As if we haven't got enough burdens already. *Chei!* What have we done to our *Chi* to deserve this fate?'

Yes indeed! What has she done to deserve this? How could Khalid, who had wooed her so ardently, humiliate her so cruelly? Look at her now - a reject, alone, when once she'd had a houseful of servants and three strong sons who loved her as much as she cherished them. How could they ban her from seeing her own sons, telling her to stay away so as not to upset them? Who would cuddle little Kene when he has a nightmare? How could Khalid reject their children for that whore of Babylon? Is this what life is all about, to give everything and end up with nothing? What's the use, then? Why bother with all this pain? Who cares? Is there even a God? What kind of

God would allow this kind of injustice on a faithful devotee? Or was Jesus punishing her for turning her back on Him for Allah, even though she'd abandoned that religion as soon as she left Khalid's house? So, if there was no forgiveness of sin, then what's the use of life? What's the use...what's the use?

*****

In death, Hadiza achieved what she couldn't in her brief lifetime - the long-awaited visit from her ex-husband. Khalid defied Latoya's objections and attended her funeral with their sons and clan members. He sensed the hostility of her family, who blamed him for her suicide. He stared at the wasted corpse in the open coffin, unable to reconcile it with the obese wife he had discarded almost a year gone. He could see the pain she had been through in the abundance of grey hair on her head, lush curls previously revealed only for his pleasure while she was his wife. Hadiza looked so pitiful in death that he felt his throat constrict, unable to suppress the sudden wetness in his eyes. *He hadn't known what she was going through. No one had said anything.* Insha'Allah! *He would have done something had he known. It was all the whore's fault. She had blinded him with her witchery and turned him into an outcast amongst his people, while doing nothing to make him less of an outcast amongst her own people. He needed to belong to his people once again, regain his roots and dignity which his good wife, Hadiza, had given him. He had stupidly cast away the one good thing in his life and now it was too late to make amends.*

Khalid let the tears flow unashamedly down his cheeks. His open grief struck a chord with the mourners and their hostility turned to sympathy. The men beat their chests in commiseration and the women clasped his hands, calling him by his peer title, *"Ogbunigwe!" machine-gun that kills in hundreds*. His sons, seeing their father's tears, finally let him into their hearts again and that night, Khalid took his children back to the house he shared with Latoya for the very first time.

But Latoya would not have them. She would not play mother to another woman's children, dead or alive. She didn't tell the fool to kill herself so why should she be burdened with her responsibilities? It was either the children or her.

This time, Khalid chose his children. He took them away from Latoya's luxury home and moved back into the dust-coated house he'd once shared with their late mother, Hadiza. Latoya's callousness to his children on the day they buried their mother finally freed him from her carnal hold. He would divorce her and devote his life to being a good father to his sons; make up for all the months of neglect and irresponsibility, *Insha'Allah.*

The house had been cleaned up by the maids from his uncle Ezekiel's house but it was a rushed job. There was still a heavy coating of dust on the furniture and an atmosphere of abandonment pervaded the large, plushly-furnished rooms with their ornate chairs and imported chandeliers. The house felt strange, yet familiar and the children wandered from room to room, touching things, talking in hushed tones unnatural for their age…remembering, mourning. The walls were still adorned with pictures, family pictures of himself, Hadiza and the children, photos from a time they were still a happy family, their smiles wide and clear, without a hint of the tragedy that was to befall them.

Khalid felt a hard knot in his chest, a lump that crawled to his throat, painful, uncomfortable. He gently turned the pictures of Hadiza to the wall as was customary when a person died. It was something he should have done from the first day he received the news of her death. But the house wasn't in use then and he didn't know there were still any photos of her in the house. He prayed it wasn't too late, that her confused spirit hadn't found its way into her pictures and became earth-bound as could happen at times.

With a deep sigh, he made his way to his former private quarters upstairs, his steps heavy. As he entered his living room, the wall clock struck 11'oclock, an hour to midnight. Khalid glanced at the clock, surprised it was still working. He flicked his wrist to confirm the time on his diamond-encrusted Rolex. *Five minutes difference*. He chose the truth of his Rolex. *A Rolex never lies.*

From somewhere down the long corridor, he heard the house-servants putting the children to bed, their voices muted, distant. Stretching out on the soft deep rug in the otherwise bare room, Khalid felt a heavy weariness descend on him. It had been a long and harrowing day. He desperately needed the warm, soft touch of a woman. *But not that whore, Latoya. Never again.* He would have to marry another wife, a decent woman this time, to take care of both his loins and the offspring of his loins, presently asleep in their old bedroom.

The sudden ringing of his mobile phone jarred the mournful silence of the house. He picked it up and answered. It was Latoya, her voice cold, hard. She wanted him back at their house that night otherwise it was goodbye forever. Khalid swore an obscene oath. That was fine by him, he told her. He'd had enough of their farcical marriage and her ridiculous friends anyway. He hung up on her and returned to his rug. He was done being a lapdog to that American whore.

His mobile rang a second time, almost an hour later, five minutes to midnight. He knew it was Latoya even before looking at the caller-id. *He'll be damned if he took her call again. She can deal with his lawyers from now on.* The phone went on ringing and he started getting really annoyed. *Bitch woman didn't care if she kept his children awake on the night they buried their mother. It was always about her...everything was always about Latoya. Well, he would soon tell her where to get off.*

He answered the call with an angry "fuck off". But Latoya was hysterical, her voice incoherent. She was screaming so loud he could barely make out what she was saying.

'Khalid, she's here! Oh my God…Khaliiid!! Help! Stay away from me….Oh Jesus! Khaliid…'

He heard a clattering sound and knew Latoya's mobile had dropped to the marbled floor of her bedroom. He could still hear the sounds coming from her room; running feet…screams in the background. Then he heard a voice that caused his blood to freeze, almost forcing the hot piss down his kaftan - Hadiza's voice, clear and strong, as if she were in the same room with him.

'You infidel whore! Unclean daughter of a pig!' Khalid heard the terrible curse spill through the line. He felt a shiver run through his body again, peppering his skin with goosebumps. He pressed the mobile tighter against his ear, his hand sweaty and hot. *It was Hadiza's voice.* He was certain…yet… it was Hadiza's voice as he'd never heard it before; harsh, hard, with a terrible resonance that sent his heart racing so fast he struggled to breath.

'You turned my husband against me, you cowardly thief of the night. Whore of Babylon! May your soul rot in eternal hell! A thousand nights of pain shall be your lot. The sharp knives of torture shall pierce your wicked heart forever. My fate shall be yours as my husband has become yours. Pig! Dog! Whore!'

Latoya's blood-curdling screams drowned out the piercing sound of Hadiza's venom. Then absolute silence. Nothing…

'Latoya!' Khalid shouted into the mobile, even as a part of his mind still functioning told him she couldn't hear him, would never hear him again; that in all likelihood, she was dead. He gripped the mobile tightly, listening…hearing nothing but the loud thudding of his heart. His body was trembling like leaves caught in a midday thunderstorm and his thoughts would not heed the reasoning of his mind - *It's not possible…It's not Hadiza…she's dead…buried…it can't be Hadiza... No way... Latoya is okay. Just fine. It's a trick...her way to get me back to the house by any means...fighting dirty as usual. I won't fall for her tricks...not this time. I won't... Yet... that voice... Hadiza's voice...*

He knew his wife's voice as well as he knew his own. He would recognise it anywhere and Latoya had never met Hadiza...No way could she imitate Hadiza's voice...no way would she use the language he'd heard in the mobile.

Like one stung by a scorpion, Khalid rushed to the teak cabinet, grabbing his car keys and wallet as he pushed his feet into his leather sandals. He took the stairs two at a time, his hasty flight awakening the household staff who peeped out of their bedrooms, their eyes wide with fright and curiosity.

As if pursued by demons, he drove through the deserted streets of Enugu. Bands of sweat poured down the sides of his face in the chilled air-conditioned interior of the Mercedes S-Class. His thoughts jumped inside his head like restless ants, thoughts of "what ifs" and terrifying images of what he might encounter at Latoya's apartment. *What if she was already dead and the police found him there? Would they think he'd killed her? Should he call the police...and tell them what exactly? That he thinks he heard the voice of his dead wife over the phone? That he thinks his dead wife has killed his present and soon-to-be ex-wife? Ha! He'd be lucky to be kept out of the psychiatric hospital with such twaddle.*

At the numerous police check-points he encountered, Khalid gave out wads of Naira notes to ensure he wasn't delayed by unnecessary searches by the policemen. They were supposed to keep the city safe by searching vehicles and drivers to prevent armed robbery and kidnapping. But everyone knew it had become a money-making scheme for the police. Bribe them with enough money and you escape detection, be you Robin Hood or the greatest train robber in the world.

As he drove up to the shut gates of Latoya's lavish residence in the exclusive area of Independence Layout, Khalid kept his palm on the horn till the panicked *Megad* dashed out of the small security house to let him in. On seeing the master of the house, a look of terror flashed through the man's face.

'What is the matter?' Khalid barked at him. 'Where is your mistress? Is everything okay?'

The *Megad* gave a mute nod but Khalid was already speeding off the long driveway towards the front entrance of the mansion. *Whatever had happened, he would soon find out for himself.* He noticed that all the lights in the house were on, as well as the external security floodlights. The compound was illuminated like a carnival fairground. Under their glare, he noticed a strange car parked among the fleet of luxury Mercedes Benz cars he'd purchased for Latoya with the notion that like a Rolex, a Merc is forever. He barely gave the car a second thought as he rushed through the doors, past the startled faces of the house servants and up the wide staircase to the private quarters of his wife.

It was only as he paused outside the closed door of Latoya's room, his heart pounding and his mouth dry, that he realised he was clutching his prayer Rosaries in his fist. He couldn't recall picking it up but Allah in His great mercy must have seen something that would necessitate the protection of the Rosary and guided his hand to it. Khalid began to mouth the ritual litany of prayers to each Rosary, praying for Allah's protection in the face of the unknown lying behind the shut door of Latoya's room. He heard hushed voices behind him and turned to see the frightened faces of the house servants.

'What is going on here?' he demanded for the second time that night. 'Is your Madam alright?'

For a brief second, the servants looked at each other before returning their gaze to him. He read something in their eyes, something shifty and fearful, yet malicious. The head servant, Ifeoma, a fat indolent woman in her early thirties, finally spoke up.

'*Oga,* master, we don't know what is happening in Madam's room,' Ifeoma said, her voice a combination of obsequiousness and fear. Khalid had never liked the woman but knew that for whatever reason, Latoya placed an unhealthy amount of trust in her. 'We hear screams from dey room but Madam not open dey door when we knock. But everything go quiet again so we think Madam gone sleep.'

Khalid gave a curt nod and sent them off to their quarters. Squaring his shoulders, he turned the knob of the thick panelled oak door. The door opened, swinging inwards with a quiet whirr to reveal the white brilliance of the opulent room. Khalid stepped inside…

And froze.

On the King-size four poster bed in his wife's room lay a nude elderly Caucasian man, dead. His lifeless eyes stared in frozen terror at an invisible horror now beyond the boundaries of his existence. His expensive shoes and clothes littered the cool tiled flooring of the vast bedroom and his mobile phone, wallet and keys were scattered on the bedside table with his open packet of Benson & Hedges. Khalid couldn't see any sign of blood on the man or any murder weapon. But there was no doubt in his mind that the man was dead.

Khalid felt his senses real as he paused to take in the scene. *Chineke! What on earth was going on? Latoya! Where was Latoya!* His eyes scanned the all-white décor of the room and found Latoya crouched against the mirrored doors of the vast wardrobes running the length of the far-side wall. Khalid felt his heart lurch at the sight of his wife, horror crawling up his spine with thin frozen fingers.

Unlike her dead lover, Latoya was partially clothed in an expensive but blood-splattered negligee. And she was alive, if one could truly describe the pathetic creature on the floor as living. Her eyes were wide…wild…like a caged hyena in a zoo. And her face… *Chineke! Her face…*

Khalid stared in stunned disbelief, shock and terror numbing his mind. Latoya's face was covered with deep bloody gorges, scratches that could only have been inflicted with talons, a tiger's claw. The injuries resembled a carefully designed artwork of a maniac, both in their precision and execution, ensuring that no part of Latoya's face went unmarked. But for her body and the fact that he knew he was in her bedroom, Khalid would have been unable to recognise the horror he beheld. *Who would have hated Latoya so much to do this to her, disfigure her so viciously? Hadiza?* He felt a shudder run through his body as he quickly pushed away the thought and slowly made his way towards his wife.

As he drew closer, he heard her low whimpers, sounds that sounded like a puppy trapped by a wild Tomcat. He saw something on the floor that made his breath catch, trapping the air in his lungs and sending his heart racing once again. *God...Allah! Would the horror never end?* By Latoya's bare feet were bloody clumps of rich black hair, Latoya's once luxurious curls, pulled with malevolent force from her scalp. Khalid could see the blood already beginning to mat on her near-bald scalp and fresh blood trickled down her forehead, beside her ears, merging with the bloody mess of her savaged face. *What kind of monster could have done this evil,* Khalid wondered, stooping low beside his wife.

Latoya looked through him, her eyes bereft of recognition. All he could see in her gaze was terror, pure unadulterated terror beyond anything he could describe. He shook her, cajoled, and threatened. But she would not speak…could not speak. He stood up to get her clothes from the wardrobe and make her decent before he drove her to the hospital and called the police.

It was then that the smell hit him, assailing his nostrils with its familiar but now terrifying scent. It was the smell of incense, the familiar fragrance of his dead wife

Hadiza, now pervading the bedroom of his living wife. Latoya's *Must de Cartier* perfume, the usual scent of her room, was swallowed by the suffocating smell of Hadiza's incense.

Khalid froze, his limbs turned to baby pap, soft, weak. His head was swimming, sending waves of terror coursing through his body. *Oh God! Allah, help me!* He cast his eyes wildly around the room, feeling the tremors quake his limbs and the shivers chill his spine. The smell was everywhere, getting stronger, suffocating, sending him rushing towards the door of Latoya's bedroom, heedless of the dead man and comatose woman in the room. All he knew was that he had to get out of that room fast. He had to get out of that house without delay.

At the staircase, he encountered Ifeoma, the head house servant. He forced himself to stop, control his erratic breathing and address her. Except she was already speaking before he could say a word, her voice urgent, pleading.

'*Oga*, I swear, we never see dey White man before. I gone call you and tell you madam get boyfriend if I knew. Please sir, don't sack us because we not know anything, I swear.'

Khalid stared at the woman boggle-eyed. *What the hell was she on about?* Then he remembered. The dead White man on the bed - Latoya's lover - definitely well-known to the slimy bitch in front of him. He didn't for one second believe that she and the rest of the servants were ignorant of his wife's indiscretions. He'd had his suspicions but never any concrete proof till tonight. A dead proof.

'Phone the police immediately and tell them to come to the house. Go and dress your mistress before the police arrive. Tell the police to come to my house if they need to speak to me. I will deal with you all later.'

'*Oga,* we don't know address of your house,' Ifeoma said.

Of course she wouldn't know. Up till tonight, he had lived in this house, shared it with Latoya, albeit in different bedrooms. He told her to give his phone number instead to the police. Without a backward glance, he drove out of the compound with the same speed he had arrived, but for entirely different reasons.

*****

Four days later, he was arrested by the police for the murder of his wife's lover and her attempted murder. His arrest was a culmination of several factors, chief amongst them, the fuss raised by the American embassy about their two citizens and the damning testimony of the house servant, Ifeoma, who swore that Khalid had killed his wife's lover before rushing out of the house. As Latoya was still in a state of shock and unable to give a statement, the police eventually yielded to the pressure from the American Embassy and arrested Khalid. He had managed to keep himself away from jail pending trial by bribing the police commissioner. But that didn't stop the local media from having a field day at his expense. After all, it wasn't every day that an illiterate Moslem millionaire killed the white lover of his American wife and left her disfigured for life, all on the same day he buried an ex-wife. Worse, he had no alibi and his story was so farfetched that it became the gag of every stand-up comedian on television - *Dear wife, how can you cheat on me with the dead white man I accidentally found on your bed? Ha! Ha!*

He tried to see Latoya, to speak with her and find out what exactly happened in her bedroom on that fateful night. He was as curious as the rest of the public despite having his own suspicions. But the police wouldn't let him anywhere near his wife; there would be no interfering with the prime witness. They had the American Embassy to consider and therefore, despite Khalid's generous bribes, couldn't accommodate him. They were really sorry and hoped he wouldn't take it personally.

He took it personally; very personally. But there was nothing he could do except read his leather-bound Koran and pray that Allah would come to his aid.

Allah did.

A week after the attack, the results of the autopsy on the white man showed that he had died of a massive coronary thrombosis that was as sudden as it was deadly. The man had a history of heart attacks and Khalid was removed as a suspect in his death. His good fortune seemed to hold when Latoya finally recovered enough to give a statement, an implausible account of temporary insanity after witnessing the sudden death of her lover, leading to her own self harm. The police did not believe her story in its entirety but she was insistent on Khalid's innocence. Her statement exonerated Khalid and turned him into the darling of the media. He went from being the illiterate murderous villain to the innocent cuckolded husband of an American whore and the victim of bullying at the hands of the American Embassy. *Who were these foreigners anyway to interfere with the great Nigerian justice system, even if they were the superpower of the world?* Messages of support flooded in from all over the country and once again, Khalid became a man of respect.

In the end, he didn't need to divorce Latoya. She divorced him, leaving the country with the speed of antelopes escaping a wild bush fire. She neither called him nor answered his calls and she made no financial demands on him. It was as if she wanted nothing to do with him - ever again; as if she had been scared witless by something she was determined to forget. Her silence left a lot of unanswered questions for Khalid, answers that would have stopped his disquieting nightmares and cured his incessant need to look over his shoulders, especially whenever he smelt the terrifying fragrance of burning incense.

*****

The nightmares had started from that night he discovered Latoya's mutilated face and fled the house in terror. At first, he thought it was his subconscious thoughts surfacing in his dreams, vivid and distorted dreams of his late ex-wife, Hadiza. He would wake up from the dreams shaking, his heart pounding, his ears still ringing with her voice, soft, insidious…chilling. He could never recollect the details of the nightmares, just flashing images, unpleasant and repulsive, like the slimy touch of something rotten and unwholesome. But he heard her voice; *he remembered her voice.* And it was a voice that sent the cold fingers of terror down his spine, causing him to dread night-time as much as he dreaded his bed.

Finally, he contacted a revered Imam, who in turn referred him to the powerful *Marabout*, Sidi Brahim. Sidi Brahim was renowned in the Moslem communities for his powerful amulets which conferred invisibility to their wearers, making them invincible to their enemies. Armed robbers sought his help to cloak them from police detection while top politicians paid him a fortune to ensure their success at the polls. When Khalid explained his troubles to the holy man, he had demanded a cow the size of an elephant. Khalid had spent a near fortune buying such a mammoth cow and when Sidi Brahim saw the cow, he gave a wide smile of approval and assured Khalid that his troubles were about to end.

That night, the Marabout followed Khalid back to his house, together with three of his acolytes. The men spent several hours digging a hole the depth of two graves. Sidi Brahim instructed that the live cow be placed into the giant grave. Then the men proceeded to Hadiza's village, several miles away, bribing their way through several police road-blocks and military checkpoints. They made their way to Hadiza's deserted graveside and began their frenzied digging once again. The acolytes were exhausted by this time. But they had seen the wads of *Naira* notes

Khalid had laid out for each of them. They would dig till they collapsed as long as they collected their prize.

When Hadiza's coffin was finally opened, Khalid refused to look into the muddied and crumbling wooden box. But his imagination saw more than his open gaze would have seen and his nose smelt the cloying stench of maggot-infested flesh…the smell of death and decay. He stumbled away from the grave, leaving the Marabout to his gruesome task. Still, his mind would not rest, building images of such horror that he thought he would go insane with fear.

As he waited for the men in his car, he kept glancing behind, jumping at every sound, his heart thudding as hard as his aching head. The owl's hoot, the bat's screech, the cricket's chirps and the occasional barking from a bored dog all had made him almost piss on himself. He nearly collapsed with relief when Sidi Brahim finally re-appeared, carrying a small bag in his hand. When Khalid asked him what the bag contained, the holy man frowned and instructed Khalid to drive back to his house in silence.

It was almost dawn when they arrived back to Khalid's compound. The Marabout retraced his steps to the grave containing the cow. The cow was in a state of extreme agitation, shoving itself against the narrow walls of the grave, mooing pitifully into the dark skies above. Khalid worried that it might wake his children up. It was a good thing he had given his *Megad* the night off otherwise, who knows what stories the security man would have carried.

The Marabout and his acolytes were soon deep in prayers and chants, circling the grave several times during the course of their invocations. Khalid was made to kneel down at the edge of the hole, while the Marabout poured some liquid over his head. It felt warm and sticky and when he wiped the trickle by his ear, Khalid's hand was stained a bright red. He could not tell whether it was chicken blood or human blood he felt.

As the Marabout exposed the contents of his bag, Khalid felt his heart stop. On the ground was a human hand, severed from the wrist. The skin was death-black and peeling, a wedding band still attached to the third finger – *Hadiza's hand!* Khalid felt the bile rise to his throat, his head swimming so fast he feared he would tumble into the deep hole that housed the mammoth cow. By Hadiza's severed hand were other personal bits of her - her grey hair, withered flesh from her cheeks, a singular tooth, white as chalk and bits of her wrapper, browned by corpse fluid.

Sidi Brahim proceeded to make a deep cut in Khalid's thumb, squeezing the thick blood over the pieces of his dead wife, all the while shouting incantations. At his command, the acolytes chucked the bloodied items into the grave atop the live cow. The animal became even more distressed, throwing itself about, its eyes wild and terror-infused.

'Bury the cow now,' the Marabout instructed, his voice cold, his face remote. Yet again, the acolytes began their nefarious chore, chucking large chunks of earth into the grave, their movements frantic, even manic, as if they couldn't wait to be done with the job.

'Hurry! Hurry, before she escapes!' the Marabout shouted at them, his voice urgent and loud. 'Come; help them,' he said to Khalid, joining his assistants. Khalid wasn't sure who the "she" was, his late wife or the sacrificial cow. He didn't want to know.

Soon, he was pouring with sweat, his heart racing with the unfamiliar physical exertion. Sidi Brahim's white kaftan was also stained a dirty brown, same as his helpers' but they didn't seem to mind. The cow's terrified moans were so loud now that they feared detection. The damp earth kept heaving with the cow's desperate struggles. Khalid felt himself shudder as he listened to the cow's mooing fade into the night, buried alive with the pieces of Hadiza. He never would've believed a cow could sound so human had he not heard the sounds himself. He knew he would never forget that terrible cry for as long as he lived.

In no time, the grave was completely filled up with earth and payment made to the Marabout and his acolytes. Khalid drove them back the thirty mile distance to their village, returning later that morning with Sidi Brahim's guaranteed assurance that his nightmares were now a thing of the past. Hadiza's spirit had been bound and buried inside the live cow and she would never haunt his dreams again. And that night, for the first time since his ex-wife died, Khalid slept the sweet dreamless sleep of a new born baby.

*****

Khalid married his third wife exactly two years to the date Hadiza died. In that period, he had reaped the joyful fruits of Sidi Brahim's work. His sleep was undisturbed, deep and dreamless. The unsettling smell of incense that had dogged his every step had vanished from both his cars and his house. It had been a long time since he had looked over his shoulders in dread, always expecting to see a presence that was never there, yet, constantly felt. His declining health gradually improved and his business flourished once again. The only aspect of his life that gave him cause for concern was his sons' progress, both at home and at school. The children's results were so abysmal that he'd resorted to bribing the teachers to ensure their grades were improved. Never having obtained an education himself, he was determined to ensure his sons would not suffer the indignities of being illiterate in an Igbo society that laid great store in education. In the end, he decided a get himself a wife, a young bride that would dedicate her time rearing his sons and warming his bed.

He married a young girl from his village, Oluchi, who at just nineteen years was perfect for his needs. Oluchi was from a poor family who were happy to marry her off to the much older Khalid once he built them a one-storey house for her dowry. This time, Khalid did not get any objections from his uncle Ezekiel or his clansmen over his choice of a bride. Soon, the wine-carrying ceremony was done and Khalid was finally free to bring his new bride back to his house.

He had renovated his private quarters in preparation, turning it into a boudoir fit for an Arab prince. Soft cushions, heavily-scented silk flowers and exotic luxury rugs adorned the huge room and soft candles and fragrant oils burnt in the corners. Gleaming Benin bronze artefacts and imported Italian chandeliers intermingled in a perfect blend of ancient and modern. The stupendously large circular bed in the centre of the room completed the opulence of his Arabian Nights' bedchamber.

Later that night, after his final Salat, Khalid groomed himself meticulously for the consummation of his marriage. He doused himself in Paco Rabane aftershave and donned his flowing white kaftan over his body. He hurried to his bedroom, humming a soft tune under his breath. He knew his new bride was already in his chambers, oiled and scented, awaiting his arrival. He paused briefly outside his bedroom to adjust his kaftan and still his racing heart, turbo-charged by passion and anticipation. Slowly, he turned the knob and pushed open the door.

Khalid gagged, stumbling backwards, his heart pounding so hard he could barely breathe. He stared around him wildly, his eyes wide with terror. From the open doorway of his bedroom, the suffocating smell of Hadiza's incense drifted into the corridor, slowly infusing the wide hall with its cloying sweetness.

For several minutes, Khalid hovered in the corridor, his back pressed to the wall, willing his heart to slow its pace, seeking his deserted man-heart. *There had to be a rational reason for the smell; a simple explanation which had nothing whatsoever to do with Hadiza. Sidi Brahim had guaranteed her exorcism and he could testify to the success of that occult procedure.*

Khalid concluded that his new wife was a lover of the same incense that his late wife had loved; just a mere coincidence, albeit an unpleasant one. That particular incense must be a popular scent amongst women, he decided. But Oluchi would have to do without it. That was one aroma he was determined to do without in his house.

Taking a deep breath, Khalid made his way back into the room, wiping his sweaty palms on his kaftan. From across the room, he saw the covered contour of his new bride on the bed. She had pulled the sheet right over her head, making herself completely invisible to his eyes. He smiled at her modesty, non-the-less pleased by it. As he made his way to the bed, he pulled off his sandals and kaftan. Placing his mobile phone and Rolex Oyster watch on the side cabinet, he stretched out on the bed alongside his new bride.

Again, he forced himself not to choke. The pungent smell of incense was even more overpowering than ever. It was as if his new bride had bathed herself in the damned thing.

'Oluchi,' he said, trying to stifle the annoyance in his voice. *After all, the poor girl wasn't to know that he had an aversion to the blasted scent*. 'I want you to get rid of the scent you use after today, okay? I don't like it one bit and would prefer that you use something different, okay?'

Khalid waited for her response but she said nothing; neither nodded her head in assent nor turned to face him. It was as if he hadn't spoken, as if she hadn't heard him. *Chineke! Surely, the silly girl hadn't fallen asleep on her own wedding night!* Insha' Allah! *He'll teach her a lesson in wifely duties if she has.* He shook her, pulling the silk cover off her head, seeing the sleek perm of her hair before turning her around to face him.

And his blood froze into hard ice. Waves of terror bathed his body in chills, causing his skin to break out in bumps. He opened his mouth to scream but the sound stuck behind his throat, choking him, causing his eyes to roll back in their sockets. He wanted to run, to jump from the bed and flee. He saw himself flying, leaping to safety from the open window of his bedroom. But his limbs were glued to the bed as he stared into the glittering cold eyes of his dead wife, Hadiza.

'Husband of my heart, father of my sons, don't you love me anymore?' The ghoul asked, its voice soft, insidious…chilling. Just as she had asked him over and over in his nightmares before Sidi Brahim bound her soul to the live cow. Except that he'd never remembered his dreams, never recalled her words - till now. *Our Lord, impose not on us afflictions which we have not the strength to bear. And pardon us! And grant us protection! Have mercy on me...have mercy on me! Oh almighty Allah! The Beneficent...the Merciful! Master of the day... and night! Have mercy on us and grant us your protection...grant us your protection...*

Khalid heard the words ring silently inside his head…over and over…as he squeezed his lids, shutting out the horror, hoping for Allah's miraculous deliverance. He felt the cold clamminess of her touch as she pulled his head down…slowly, unresisting…to her cold, cold lips!

And the spell broke. Khalid reeled back in revulsion, falling out of the bed, knocking his head against the hard wood of the bedside cabinet. He was moaning, whimpering like a day-old puppy as his manhood became undone in an undignified puddle of hot piss. He heard the rustling of silk as the spectre rose from the bed, seeming to float towards him in a terrifying soundless motion. Abstractly, his mind registered the beautiful silk of her negligee, a bridal lingerie, expensive, sensual and light. He saw that the body beneath it was lithe, supple and shapely. But he knew that the truth lay in the eyes, the petrifying gaze of his ex-wife, Hadiza, bloodless, icy and dead…*Chineke Nna...* Very dead.

He tried to back away, his movements clumsy, frantic. But she was everywhere, behind him, in front of him, at his left and at his right. There was no escape and Allah was not hearing his desperate supplications. He crouched low, shielding his head beneath his arms. His body trembled like dancing leaves caught in a tropical storm and sweat poured in rivulets down his exposed body. He knew his day of reckoning had finally arrived. Hadiza would get her vengeance on him for his betrayal and the mutilation of her corpse by Sidi Brahim.

Suddenly, he heard a scream, a cry of such agony that his head snapped up from its refuge beneath his arms. Khalid saw yet more horror that nearly made his wits desert him for good. His new bride, Oluchi, was standing before him, goring her face with her pink-polished nails. Over and over she scratched, digging her nails into her skin, reaching deeper and harder till her silk bridal negligee was covered in her scarlet blood. And all the while she screamed, squealed like a pig being butchered with a blunt knife. But she seemed incapable of stopping the self-mutilation, her eyes wild, tears pouring from them, pleading for him to save her from herself.

Khalid jumped up and grabbed her bloody hands, pinning them to her side, keeping them away from her face. Instantly, they went limp in his hands, all fight gone from them. Her body shook as if hammered by a quake, her movements spasmic and violent. He folded her in his arms, holding her tight, trying to quell her tremors. He whispered hushed words of comfort into her sleek permed curls, his voice as unsteady as her body. For a while, it seemed as if his efforts were in vain as she continued to wail and tremble, her voice choked with pain.

Then, she stopped crying. Her sobs cut off like a CD paused in mid-play. Khalid felt a sudden chill seeping through the silk of her lingerie, sending the shivers to his bare skin. He remembered his state of undress, compounded by his piss-dampened underwear. He let go of his new bride. He needed to make himself decent before discussing what just took place with Oluchi.

But she held unto him with almost superhuman strength, her arms like metal bands around his waist. *The poor girl was afraid, terrified out of her wits and who would blame her,* he thought. She would have many questions and he had no explanations that would make any sense to anyone. More importantly, she would need medical attention for her facial injuries and he dreaded the rumour mill when it emerged that yet another wife had been disfigured in his house.

He tried again to extricate himself from her hold but she held on tight. His teeth were beginning to chatter from the chill and his body grew numb with each passing second.

'Husband of my heart, father of my children, don't you love me anymore?' Her voice was soft…chilling, muffled against his bare chest.

This time, Khalid did not fight the terror. It engulfed him and imprisoned his mind as completely as his body was being crushed in the grip of his dead wife's arms. He was losing consciousness, his breath dying out and his limbs becoming insubstantial, unable to hold up his heavy frame. The tightness in his chest felt as if a ten-tonne truck was crushing him beneath its wheels. He tried to raise his hands to his chest, to release the relentless grip on it. But his arms were like lead, heavy and useless.

The chill seeped right through to his bones, turning his body into a hulking lump of ice. Pin-dots of dazzling light darted around him, blinding him, coating his pupils with sightlessness. *No man can escape his Karma. Sooner or later, we all have to pay. Hadiza, I'm sorry…so sorry…*

And Khalid gave in to the crushing chill, as the darkness of hades engulfed him in final eternal oblivion.

THE RETURNED

'Oh God...what a bloody silly way to die...'
(Daphne Du Maurier – Don't Look Now)

(Amaka)

I was driving along a narrow potholed road just before the busy *Agbani* junction, when I first saw the child. On the other hand, maybe it was the car I saw first, the big gleaming black Mercedes Benz that took up most of the road, forcing me to swerve a sudden stop by the dusty side-path to avoid a collision with the speeding car.

'*Anu ofia! Animal!*' I shouted the obscenity, turning furious eyes towards the reckless driver. It was then that I saw the child, a little boy, eight or nine years at the most, waving, banging desperately on the tinted window of the back seat of the Merc. His eyes were wild with terror, tears drenching his face. I had a daughter, my little girl, *Adaora,* who could well be the same age as the little boy I'd glimpsed through that opaque pane. Therefore in an instant, I read the tears of that child - terror…pure unadulterated fright; the kind a child cries for night terrors rather than bruises and falls.

Without a second's thought, I did a U-turn, my driving now as reckless as the Merc driver's. I fired up my trusty Peugeot, hoping its speed would do the job – *not that a Peugeot would ever be a match for a Mercedes Benz but I would give it my very best*. I was getting close to the busy

Agbani Road Junction and hoped the usual heavy traffic would somehow delay the Merc and buy me time.

I was lucky. I spied the black beast about five cars in front of me, caught in the slow-moving traffic just as I'd hoped. I pulled into the busy road, hearing the angry curses of an irate male driver, something about incompetent women drivers. *Sexist idiot*. I tried to manoeuvre my car closer to the Merc but the road was almost gridlocked with traffic, pedestrians, hawkers and beggars. I beeped my horn several times as I tried to get myself nearer to my target. *Come on, come on!*

I saw the Merc pull out of the queue, no doubt, intending to escape with what I now suspected was his kidnapped victim. No father would drive so recklessly with their small son in the car and no child would wear such terror in the presence of its father. I instantly mimicked the action of the Merc, swerving and weaving my way through cars and *Okada* motorbike taxis. I heard other drivers slam their horns in protracted angry beeps; saw others swerve dangerously to avoid collision with my car and the Merc. I wondered that no one else had spied what I'd seen through those tinted windows and made chase.

I caught up with the Merc at a fortuitous junction, just before the dual-carriageway of the *Trunk A* Express Road. Unbelievably, I was right behind him! I couldn't see the child anymore through the back window screen but *I knew* he was still there, trapped within the dark confines of that black mobile prison. Without thinking, I pressed down on my accelerator and rammed my Peugeot into the rear of the Merc, feeling my neck jerk violently from the impact. Then I was out of my car, running towards the Merc, rapping on the driver's wound-up window, all the while searching for the petrified child inside.

Then I saw him again, the little boy, but this time crouched on the floor of the car. He lifted his head briefly and once again I felt my heart race with fury-induced adrenalin. *Any monster that could do this to a child deserved to die.* I heard the soft whirr of the driver's window as the lunatic finally wound down the tinted glass. I stared into an overblown coal-hued face, covered in tribal marks that cut deep ridges on both sides of his cheeks. The man was clearly a stranger to our parts. We Igbos didn't practice the habit of facial scarring popular with most other tribes in the country. *The bastard devil-man thought he could just drive into our town and kidnap one of our children with impunity? Well, he had another think coming.*

'I want you to give me that child at once, you bloody kidnapper,' I yelled, noticing a couple of cars pulling up around us and emboldened by the prospect of their support. I saw the sudden fury in the blood-shot eyes of the man; saw the bitter hatred before I finally saw the gun in his right hand. Then I heard a loud report which temporarily killed my eardrums. I felt a dull pain on the left side of my breast and felt myself falling down…down…till I hit the black asphalt road, which was hot against my arm, baked by the blazing mid-day sun. *Chineke! I've been shot! Nnem oohh! My Mother! Who will care for my little daughter?*

I reached for my chest with trembling hands, feeling for my wound. But I felt no pain! And when I raised my hand to my gaze, I saw no blood! The bullet had missed me after all! *Thank you Jesus! Chei! God's miracles know no bounds!* I jumped up from the ground, pulling down my silk blouse to protect my modesty. Then, I ran back towards the Merc, which was now starting to pull away. I managed to yank open the back door, flinging myself unto the white leather seat just as the car sped away. The man glanced back and frowned at me, his fleshy face sleek with hot sweat, his smile as evil as the gun I spied lying on the front passenger seat. The little boy stared at me, his eyes tear-soaked, wide as a night owl's. He whimpered as I pulled him onto the seat by me, folding him in my arms.

'Shut up!' The fat lunatic at the wheel growled, again glancing over his shoulder at us before turning back to the road. 'Who tell you to get up from the floor, eh?' He yelled at the child, his voice as ugly as his face. The boy sunk deeper into the curve of my arms, burying his face on my thighs. I stroked his hair gently, holding him tight, wishing a slow, torturous death for our vile captor. 'Tha's better. Stay down like dat till I tell you to get up, you hear?' The devil-man turned up the music in the car and slammed his foot on the pedal. The Merc ate up the kilometres with the ease of a rocket.

I leaned down and picked up the edges of my flowered skirt. With gentle strokes, I wiped the child's face with it, smiling down at him as he lifted his face to mine.

'It's alright, my child,' I whispered, stroking his cheek. 'I will not let anything happen to you, I promise.' He nodded…a slow nod…and I saw the terror gradually ebb from his eyes… but not quite. We were still trapped in the car with our evil captor and he was a big man with a deadly gun.

'What's your name?' I whispered to the child, trying to distract him from our predicament.

'Ifeanyi,' he said. 'Ifeanyi Eze.'

'And how old are you, Ifeanyi?'

'Ten years,' his voice was still low, quivery.

'Ten years!' I put the wonder into my voice. 'That's a big boy! I have a daughter, Adaora. She's nine years old, just a year younger than you.' As I mentioned my daughter's name, I felt a sudden sadness overwhelm me, a strong feeling of loss and pain. I prayed the other passers-by who had witnessed the shooting would call the useless Police and report the incident or we'd be truly damned. It would probably be hours before I made it home to my daughter and house-maid cum nanny. She'd no doubt be worried out of her little mind but at least she was safe at home, away from harm's way, unlike this poor child, Ifeanyi, trapped in the back seat of an evil kidnapper's car.

'Ifeanyi, tell me my child; how come you ended up in this man's car?' I asked, watching his eyes pool up again. 'Shhh. It's okay. Don't cry now, okay? I promise you everything will be alright. The police will soon catch up with us, okay?' I had no idea where the devil-man was taking us but I would rather die than let any harm come to this poor child who now looked at me with the unquestioning trust of a loyal dog.

'I was standing outside our school gate waiting for our driver when he came and said my mummy asked him to bring me home because our car has spoilt,' Ifeanyi's low voice broke into my thoughts. *Dear Jesus!* Bastard kidnappers always used the same ploy! One would think that by now, parents would know to warn their kids about such stranger danger. But obviously not. My parents hadn't warned me about it when I was kidnapped in my seventh year as I walked to the corner kiosk to buy some sweets. Fortunately, my kidnappers, a mother and her two teenage sons, had wanted ransom money to get them out of their poverty-trapped lives. Other kidnappers wanted something more sinister, as I suspected the fat devil-man did. My kidnappers had been kind to me during the time I spent in their thatched hut in a remote tree-shrouded location. But I still remember crying incessantly, alone and frightened, missing my widowed mother and sister with a desperation that stole my appetite in my three days of captivity. I was ransomed in the end and my kidnappers were never caught. But the experience had left me wary. I never let my daughter, Adaora, leave the house on her own for any reason. From the time she could talk, I had drummed all the possible kidnap scenarios into her little head and it would be an extraordinarily ingenious kidnapper that would get Adaora to follow him *or her* as willingly as Ifeanyi had the devil-man.

'Didn't you know you must never talk to strangers or follow anyone into their car?' Ifeanyi made no response and I sighed deeply. There was no need crying over the chick that had escaped the coop. As our people say, that silly fowl would soon learn its lesson inside the boiling soup pot of a wretched and starving widow. Ifeanyi would never need any more lessons in stranger-danger if he got out of our predicament alive.

And despite my assurances, I was beginning to doubt the likelihood of our salvation, not with the way the man was speeding and the total absence of police road blocks. *Devil's luck!* When you didn't need them, the bloody police were everywhere, setting up illegal road blocks and demanding bribes from motorists. Then when you really needed them, they would suddenly become as scarce as a man on a virgin's bed.

I leaned forward and placed a tentative hand on our captor's shoulder. His neck jerked as if stung by a scorpion, a startled look in his eyes. I quickly withdrew my hand. I didn't want to offend him. Rather, I hoped to use my womanly wiles to get him to see reason. People always said how beautiful I was; how my light skin, flowing long hair and tall, slender body were enough to win me the President as a husband if I wanted. My mother had been of mixed-race parentage and my sister and I had inherited her colour and the silky lushness of her hair. The only person who hadn't been enslaved by my purported beauty was my ex-husband, who'd left me for another woman when I failed to give birth to another child after Adaora. A fibroid growth had necessitated the removal of my womb. He called me a man-woman, female on the outside, male on the inside, with the fruitless belly of a man. This insult, even though I had given birth to our daughter before the poison of fibroids soured my womb.

Despite my defect, men continued to pester me while my family urged me to remarry. But marriage held no attraction for me anymore. At least not while my daughter still needed my unshared attention. Maybe someday in the future, when time had dulled my memory and cured my insecurities.

'*Oga,* chief,' I said to the kidnapper, my voice low, submissive. 'Please sir, have mercy on this little boy. I can tell you're not an evil man.' I lied without shame. 'I'm sure you're a father and love your own children. How would you feel if someone did to your son what you're now doing to this poor innocent child?' The fat man kept his face to his tinted windscreen, his features remote, uncaring. But he heard me, alright.

'What you expect me to do, eh?' he finally said, his voice like granite, rough, yet without substance, as if he spoke into my head. 'I have only one son and ten daughters. I mus' win dey Local Government elections next month otherwise my enemies go chop my head. My *Babalawo* say dat only sacrifice of little boy will work. What you want me to do, eh? Kill my only son?'

Chineke Nna! God our father! Tufia! God forbid such evil! It was as I feared. The man was amongst the vile sect of politicians who believed in blood sacrifices for victory at the polls. No small child or woman was safe at election times while these breed of evil men walked the earth.

'Oga, sometimes these Babalawos don't know what they're saying because a lot of them are fake. I should know. My father was a well-known *Dibia* in our parts before he died. There was no kind of juju medicine he couldn't make for people and he never once used human sacrifice. He even predicted his own death, down to the very day and time, even though he didn't know how he would die. He thought perhaps his rope would break while he was climbing the palm tree to tap his palm-wine. So he did not take to the tree that morning, just to see if he could thwart death. But no man can escape his fate. He was bitten by *Echieteka,* the deadly viper, right inside his own room and died before he could prepare a cure for himself, exactly on the same day and time he had foreseen. I tell you all this sir, for you to know that I have experience of *Babalawos* and that you don't need to have this child's blood on your head just for a political post.'

I waited to see if my words had any effect on the devil-man but he ignored me and continued driving. I leaned back on my seat and took the child back in my arms.

'What did you tell him, Auntie?' Ifeanyi whispered, looking at me with his wide trust-filled eyes. *What a well brought up child! Knowing to address his elders with the respectful "Auntie".*

'Shut up behind there before I do it for you, idiot boy,' the devil-man shouted at us and Ifeanyi pressed himself against me, terror clouding his eyes once again. I rocked him gently, stroking his hair, his face, his arm.

'It's okay. He won't do anything to you, my child,' I whispered. 'Don't be afraid. He told me he has ten daughters and a little boy just like you. So, he won't do anything to another little child no matter what his *Babalawo* or anyone tells him, okay?'

Ifeanyi said nothing. I wasn't sure I had convinced him of his safety.

'What's a *Baba...Babawo,* Auntie?' Ifeanyi's voice was low.

Chei! Idiot basket-mouth woman that I am, mentioning the stupid Babalawo *to the child on top of all his other worries.*

'A *Babalawo,'* I corrected. 'A *Babalawo* is like a *Dibia*, a witch doctor,' I explained. 'He said his *Babalawo* told him to bring a little boy so he can win his Local Government election. He thinks that God will hear the prayers of little boys faster than other prayers.' This time, I was more circumspect, careful to avoid any mention of human sacrifices.

'So why won't he take his own little boy to pray for the Baba… *Babalawo*… instead of me?'

Chineke Nna! I was really roping myself in with my own lies. But it was that or scare the wits out of the child.

'I think he said his son was away on holiday somewhere or he would have used him. Now listen, why don't you shut your eyes and try to sleep, okay? I'll wake you up when we get there.'

'I don't want to sleep, Auntie. I'm hungry.'

'I know; I know, my son. Don't worry. We'll soon stop and I'll get you something to eat, okay?' Ifeanyi nodded, nestling his head deeper against my breast. *Poor little thing! Please God, Please Jesus Christ; Please save this child...Please. I promise I shall go to church every Sunday and pay up all my tithes diligently. I'll even take Adaora to visit my nasty ex-mother-in-law despite the fact that she encouraged her son to abandon our marriage. Just spare this child from this evil, please Lord.*

And God heard my prayers!

I heard the devil-man shout a loud curse and looked up to see the most wonderful sight on earth - a police road block! *Finally! Thank you Jesus!*

The devil-man did a sudden swerve, flinging us violently against the door panel. Ifeanyi bumped his knee against the window-winder and let out a pained cry. I held him closer, now fearing for our lives than ever before. Already, I could hear the police sirens wailing behind us as the devil-man sped off like the psychotic maniac he was. I recalled horror stories of trigger-happy policemen who killed victims and criminals with the same reckless zeal, disregarding every safety code in the book. It would be the greatest tragedy if we survived everything only to be killed by the very policemen that should have protected us.

'Look what you jus' do, you idiot boy,' screamed the devil-man as he tried to outrun the police vehicle. 'If you no shut up now, I go shut your mouth for you *kpata-kpata,* completely, you hear?' Ifeanyi whimpered, pressing deeper into my arms.

'Shhh...it's okay, child. It's okay. I'll not let anything happen to you. I promise.' I continued to rock him in my arms. I started humming a little song I used to sing for my daughter whenever she was down with Malaria. Adaora loved it. She called it *The Clever Lizard song.* It always brought a little smile to her fever-dampened face.

'*Kuolunu nwa ngwere aka, elente.*
Nwa Ngwere ejeghi ije, O gbara-oso, elente

Kuolunu Nwa Ngwere aka, elente.'

(Clap for the little lizard. The little lizard who didn't walk but rather, ran. Clap for that clever little lizard).

And as I sang, I felt the return of that desolate feeling; of intense pain and loss; felt my eyes pool up even as the child slowly melted against me, the tight tension easing from his shoulders. Then our car began to swerve, lurch…tilt…as burning tyres screeched and we started somersaulting down the deep tree-pebbled ravine.

Ifeanyi screamed, wrapping his little arms tightly around me. I crouched my body over him, holding him with every strength in my weak female body, feeling our world tumble upside down, inside out and everywhere and finally, nowhere…nothing.

And everything went black.

*****

(Ifeanyi)

From my work-desk in my home office, I looked out of the open window and watched my children at play. They were huddled around the double swing, my twin sons and their little sister. I saw the boys gesticulate with their arms, no doubt trying to get their sister back indoors so they could get on with their boys' stuff. *Fat chance, boys!* My little daughter always got her way, not just with her brothers but with everyone else. She neither adopted tantrums nor sulks. But there was something about her gentle ways that got everyone bending over backwards to please her.

As I watched her with her brothers, I marvelled yet again at her extraordinary difference. She could easily be mistaken for a foundling. In fact, I remember my wife's fury when she heard the rumours of her purported infidelity. People were saying our daughter couldn't possibly be mine. We are dark complexioned, my wife and I. Our twin sons are as dark-skinned as us. Yet, our daughter could almost pass for a child of mixed-blood - European and African bloodlines; such was the fairness of her skin. She was very tall for her age, almost as tall as her two brothers, who at nine years were five years her senior. A less trusting husband would indeed suspect his wife of infidelity.

I heard the high gates of my house squeak and my heart knocked a sudden lurch. I jumped up from my desk, rushing to the open window, scanning my compound with panic-widened eyes. I saw my *megad* saunter through the open gate, clutching a small plastic bag of shopping. My anxiety subsided as I watched the security-man shut and lock the gate behind him. My children, unaware of my emotions, carried on with their business, having now wandered over to the paw-paw grove. I saw my daughter break away from her brothers, running towards the kitchen, her long braids flying in the air. *Oh no! What was it this time?* It hurt my heart to see my daughter's tears. I could bear anything but her tears.

The door of my office burst open and my daughter rushed in, flinging herself into my open arms, her body shuddering in the familiar silent sobs that killed my soul. My daughter did not cry like other children did, loudly, angrily, even plaintively. Instead, she sobbed the hard soundless cries of a keening widow; a bereaved mother mourning the loss of a beloved child; a strong man confronted with the sudden violent loss of his entire clan in a tribal war. The first time I witnessed that terrible cry, she'd been just a few hours old and still inside the crib at the maternity ward. She had opened her eyes, still hazy from her prolonged sojourn in the womb and stared at me. A swift recognition passed between us. I looked at her and saw my beautiful little daughter, soft, sweet, vulnerable. But she'd looked at me and she knew me…*she knew me.*

That was when she began to cry. I saw her eyes squeeze shut, her face crumble, big balls of tears rolling down her red cheeks, her toothless mouth open in silent sobs. And something died in my heart, my joy…my peace. I stooped and picked her up, even before my wife could do so. I pressed her little head to my chest and held her to me, rocking her, soothing her with gentle words till her body stopped quivering in my arms. Minutes later when I looked down into her little face, her eyes were as clear as the pebbled stream of *Asata* and I could have sworn I saw a smile brighten her face, even though my wife insisted a new-born baby couldn't smile. I kissed her soft cheeks, nuzzling her face with mine, inhaling the sweet baby scent of pure innocence. I felt my heart flower with joy, knowing my daughter was at peace again.

And that was how it had always been between us, my gentle daughter and I. Her tears were my tears, her joys my joy. My wife had long given her up as mine, pouring all her love on her twins. Of course, she loved our daughter dearly - *who wouldn't?* But she knew that the child would always store her heart in the two palms of my hands.

'Auntie, Papa's Auntie; what's the matter, my sweet? Who has upset you?' I cooed, as I wiped her tears, lifting her to my laps and holding her close to my chest. I rocked her, willing the soundless sobs away. For several seconds, her body continued to shudder within my arms, her tears dampening the thin cotton of my shirt. I started to hum her special song, the one song that always soothed her.

> '*Kuolunu nwa ngwere aka, elente.*
> *Nwa Ngwere ejeghi ije, O gbara-oso, elente*
> *Kuolunu Nwa Ngwere aka, elente.'*
> *(Clap for the little lizard...).*

And as always, the song worked its mystical magic. I felt her quieten, felt her small body relax against mine. She stuck her thumb into her mouth and began to suck furiously.

'Auntie, remember you must never suck your dirty thumb otherwise you'll get germs and be very sick.' I gently extricated the thumb from her mouth, stroking the poor mangled limb, before reaching into my drawer to withdraw a packet of her favourite biscuits. Her eyes lit up, all sadness forgotten. She began to nibble the biscuit, humming her favourite lullaby, *The Clever Lizard* song. And as I hummed along with her, I remembered once again the first time I met my beautiful, gentle daughter and I felt my throat constrict in a painful knot.

*****

It was on the hot season of my tenth year, my last year at Our Lord The Redeemer's Primary School. *It was also the year of my famous kidnap by the evil politician from Ogun State. I remember my terror as I cowered on the floor of the car where my kidnapper had ordered me to stay. The next thing I remember was a violent shudder, as if we had hit something hard; then, looking up into the face of the most beautiful woman in the world as she spoke to my captor through the open window of his car.*

I heard the gunshot and my captor sped off, but not before the beautiful lady got into the car; Mrs Amaka Izuorah, my beautiful Auntie with the long curly hair, who held me, comforted me, talked me through my terrible ordeal and made the greatest sacrifice for me. Even now, even after all these years, the memory of that terrible day still fills my heart with indescribable pain.

I remember our ride of terror in that big car, the police chase that resulted in our crash. I remember Auntie shielding my body with her own, comforting me, promising to protect me and keep me safe. Then being lifted from the wreck of the car by the police, together with my captor...asking the police to save Auntie, who had saved my life.

Then my true horror began....

They could not find Auntie, either in the wrecked car or the surrounding bushes. Again and again, the police asked me questions about Auntie - what was her name? How did I know her? When did she join us in the car? What did we talk about? What did she look like? When, what, where, how, who....

To all their questions I gave the details. I watched again as they returned to my abductor who sat on the ground by one of the police vans, handcuffed and roughened by the beating the police had given him. Beside the man were the stacks of Naira *notes he had pulled from his multi-fold* Babariga *top, as he'd initially attempted to bribe the police. But this was one crime that even the notoriously greedy Nigerian police were not about to ignore. Crime against children in our child-loving Igbo culture was a reviled abhorrence. The policemen were most likely all fathers themselves. It could have happened to any of their sons.*

They'd beaten the man mercilessly for trying to bribe them before handcuffing him. I heard the politician try to talk his way out of trouble after his bribery ploy failed, saying he was friends with so and so State Governor...Senator...even the Deputy Vice-President. Why! *He'd even sat on the prestigious "high table" during President Bill Clinton's famed visit to Nigeria! His name-*

dropping fell on deaf ears, with one policeman making fun of him, asking him to get his "connections" to appoint him as the next Inspector General of Police and maybe…maybe they'll consider letting him go.

Finally, the evil man had attempted the "divide and rule" culture prevalent in our country, singling out the one officer he recognised as a fellow tribesman and asking him to save his "brother" from these "Okoro" *people. (*"Okoro*" being a derogatory term for* Igbo *people amongst certain other tribes in our country, due to its "John Smith" prevalence as an Igbo surname). But even his tribesman had been shamed by his despicable crime and would have nothing to do with him. If anything, he gave the man more beatings than the other police officers.*

Passers-by had parked by the roadside in ever-growing numbers, eager to see the ghoulish scene of the accident and watch the humiliation of the child abductor. People were cursing him, throwing stones at him, spitting at him and wishing him every kind of evil. I sat in the safety of the police car watching the scene, searching anxiously for Auntie, even as I wanted to just go home to my mother. The policemen came back to me in the car and said that they had questioned my abductor rigorously but he denied ever having Auntie as a passenger. They wanted to take me to him, get me to repeat my story before him and hopefully get a confession from him. I was happy to comply. The man was a liar as well as an evil kidnapper.

'You know Auntie was in the car with us,' I accused as soon as I saw him, even then, amidst the protection of the police and general public, feeling a vestige of terror as I looked into his puffy blood-shot eyes.

'Why you dey lie, eh? Why you say I carry woman with me in my car when it be jus' you and me, eh? Abi, you not get me into enough trouble already? What you want, eh? My head, eh?' I couldn't believe how convincingly the man lied.

'When Auntie touched your shoulder and talked to you, you told her you had ten daughters and a son and that your Babalawo *told you to bring a little boy so you can win your Local Government election,' I accused, my voice raised.*

I heard the crowd gasp as they grasped the full implication of my abduction. Suddenly, there was pandemonium as the people surged towards the politician, intent on jungle justice, even in the presence of the police.

But it was the man's reaction to my accusations that raised the goose bumps in my arms. He stared at me with terror-filled eyes, his fleshy lips slack like an idiot's, a loud shout escaping his lips.

'Oluwa o! *Oh my God! Dey boy na wizard; I tell you dis boy is* Mami-Water *mermaid child.* Oluwa o! Egbawa o! *I remember I feel sometin very cold, like ice water on my shoulder when I drive. I look but I not see anytin but my shoulder just dey pain me very bad since then. How dey boy know I get ten daughters and one son, eh? Ask him how he know? I never tell him anytin, I swear. How he know about my Babalawo and election? I not tell any woman anytin. Dey boy na wizard, I tell you. Oluwa o! Is God who save me from dis evil boy.'*

I noticed that people were suddenly staring at me, confusion and doubt on their faces. The evil politician was trying to make me out as the bad one, an accursed entity to be feared and distrusted by humans.

'You are a liar!' I screamed at him, tears of anger and frustration staining my cheeks. 'First, you shot your gun at Auntie when she stopped you and tried to kill her. But she jumped into the car and you saw her...you saw her! Where is Auntie? What have you done with Auntie?' I was screaming hysterically, feeling the pent-up emotions of my ordeal finally overwhelm me. One of the policemen held me back, trying to calm me, even as his colleagues turned to my abductor.

'You never told us you shot at a woman,' the policeman accused, cuffing the politician's right ear with

the butt of his rifle. The man moaned, looking ready to faint.

'It's not possible...I tell you dey boy is lying. I kill dat yellow woman dead. She jam my car with her car, tell me to give her dey boy. I jus' pick up my gun and shoot her in dey chest. She die at dey spot, I tell you. I take my two eyes see her body. No way she ride in dat car with us, no way. She don die, I tell you. The boy is lying.'

But I could see the truth dawn on the man even as he screamed at the police; saw the terror in his eyes as he turned to look over his shoulder; watched him continue to look over his shoulders as he was led away by the police. I felt a sudden terror grip my soul as I watched my abductor, feeling my skin break out in sudden goosebumps. And I knew that I would never see Auntie alive again. I also knew that the politician would always look over his shoulders till his dying day.

Even as I hugged my tearful and overjoyed mother later that evening; even as we watched the news on the television about the evil politician that had abducted a child for human sacrifice and now faced the death sentence himself; even as people talked about the brave good Samaritan that was shot by the roadside trying to save the kidnapped boy, herself a beautiful, young mother of a young child; Yes, even as all these played out around me, I held tightly unto the knowledge that Auntie had been there in that car with me when she was supposed to be dead. She had defied death to protect me, even after losing her life for my sake.

I could not talk about Auntie to anybody, not even my mother, for fear I would be branded a wizard or an Ogbanje, *spawned from the dead womb of the fearsome mermaid beneath the river Niger. But I never forgot my wonderful Auntie, not through the rest of my boyhood and teenage-hood; not through my university years and eventual fame as an author. Later, marriage and fatherhood dulled my memory of Auntie, consigned her to the deepest recesses of my mind. Until the day I picked up my little light-skinned daughter from her crib and saw the circular dark blemish beneath her left breast, marring the flawless tone of her skin; a blemish that mimicked to perfection, the scarring of a bullet wound.*

And I knew...I finally knew...

*****

I felt my daughter's restlessness as she finished her biscuit and jumped off my knees before dashing out of the room again to join her brothers at their play. I sighed, feeling suddenly bone-weary, needing a break from my writing. I heard the children's noisy squeals and walked over the open window. The twins saw me and waved. I waved back, smiling with pride. They were good boys - strong boys - who would always be protected from harm as long as God kept me alive. My daughter looked up from her game and once again, that sudden recognition passed between us. She looked at me and saw her adoring, fussy and over-protective father and I looked at her and saw her….*her*…

Again, I made my silent vow to protect her this time as she had once protected me, making the ultimate sacrifice for me on that fateful blistering day of my first meeting with her, long before her second return to our world.

NIGHT-FLYER

'You dreamed and saw yourself reborn.'
(Anne Rice – Pandora)

His heart was racing, his body twitching as he struggled to escape from the place of eternal night, the dark water-world littered with great jagged boulders and wailing sad men.

And the Blood-man.

Their wailing voices, discarnate…terrible…had sent the chills down his neck, through his bones, spiralling him back to his sleeping six-year old body in his single metal-framed bed. Ikem jerked up from his mattress, his heart pounding, his breathing harsh and loud in the small dark bedroom. *Oluwa o! What a horrible, horrible dream!* He felt drained, as if the blood-witch from Uchenna, their housemaid's folktales had sucked up all his blood. He quickly crossed himself…*in the name of the Father and the Son and the Holy Spirit, amen.* Then he flung the evil out of his body, swinging his thin arms three times over his head, his snapping fingers sharp as bullets. *Good!* That should keep away the *Amosu* night-demons, ensuring the bad dream would never return to haunt his sleep again. He reached over to his bedside lamp and turned on the switch. Nothing! *Not again! Not fair!* NEPA, the notorious Nigerian Electric Power Authority, had cut the power off again.

Ikem's wide eyes picked the shadows in the deep darkness of his room, shadows that now took on human form, oozing malevolence and spite. He quickly shut his eyes, hiding his head underneath the patterned cotton wrapper that shrouded his body. In the dark warmth of his fabric cocoon, he heard the loud snores of the housemaid cum nanny, Uchenna. He pictured her sleeping on her thin raffia mat in the family parlour and wondered whether to wake her up to light his kerosene lantern. But that would require him getting out of his bed to traverse the now dangerous and unknown terrain of his darkened bedroom, with ghosts and *Amosu* night-flyers lurking in the dark corners in wait for his blood. Worse, Uchenna would tease him mercilessly as soon as his parents were out of the house, calling him a cry baby and spreading spiteful lies about him to the other kids in the neighbourhood.

Ikem held his breath, stilling his body, straining to hear the alien sounds of spectral intruders. The tick-tock of his small wall clock sounded as loud as drums. Uchenna's raucous snores reminded him a bit of Olu's pig. *Ha! Just wait till he tells everyone tomorrow how Uchenna snores like Olu's pig. He'll get his own back on her for squealing on him that time he wet his bed when he was down with malaria.*

Uchenna was a mean housemaid, not a bit like his old housemaid Ngozi, who'd been kind and good and bought him sweets. Uchenna stole the meat from his soup bowl and threatened to abandon him on the walk back from school if he told his parents about her. He didn't like Uchenna, not even the tiniest bit. If only Mama would send her away and bring back Ngozi. But Mama said Ngozi had gone off to marry and have her own kids and Uchenna was nearer his own age, being twelve years old. She would not go off to get married for a very long time. *Huh! Who would want to marry horrid Uchenna? He wouldn't; yuck! She'll steal all her children's meat...and peanuts...and puff-puff...and moi-moi...and her husband will be very hungry and her children will cry because Uchenna had stolen all their meat and...they...*

When next Ikem awoke, the sun was streaming through his Louvre windows and Mama was shouting instructions to Uchenna. He stretched sleep-weary arms, his mouth wide in an early-morning yawn. He desperately needed to wee and the tantalising aroma of fried plantain brought the growl to his tummy. In a flash, he was out of his bed, running towards the toilet at the end of the narrow corridor, his hands clutching his groin, holding back the water that threatened to disgrace his pyjama bottoms. He barely made it in time, spreading his offering liberally between the white ceramic bowl, the black toilet seat and the linoleumed flooring of the toilet. *Ha! That will teach Uchenna when Mama gets her to clean up the toilet!*

Uchenna…something about her niggled him but he couldn't recall what it was. Just vague recollections of a restless night and darkness and meat…*Chei! He was really hungry. He could even swallow a whole pig. That was it! Uchenna snored like Olu's pig last night. Ha! Wait till he told on her!* For a brief second, a fleeting memory surfaced in his mind, something about the night…something unpleasant… Ikem didn't try hard to remember. Moreover, he was really starving and the plantain smelled enticing, bringing another loud grumble to his stomach. He rushed towards the kitchen and breakfast.

*****

Ikem wasn't sure which he hated the most; the stiff green Sunday suit and tight bow-tie which left him as hot as a roasting chicken or the lack of a weekend lie-in every Sunday. He had thought that getting older would free him from the tedious chore of Sunday service. But at ten years old, Mama still insisted on dragging him to listen to Pastor's weekly bleating, all in the name of God and sin.

Squashed between Mama and Uchenna in the packed Pentecostal church, hoping Jesus wouldn't read his sinful thoughts, Ikem wished for something drastic to happen and put an end to the intolerable torture of Sunday service. An armed robbery perhaps. There was a lot of money in the collection trays for them to steal. It was bad enough listening to Pastor Olumide screaming at witches and demons without having Uchenna's toneless screeching deafen his eardrums. He knew Uchenna deliberately leaned into his ears when she sang because she knew how much he hated her voice, the evil girl. When he tried pushing her away, Mama scowled at him and held his hand in a painful grip.

'Ikem Ani, for God's sakes, behave yourself in Jesus' house,' Mama scolded before continuing with her singing. Uchenna smirked and Ikem kicked her shin. She promptly kicked him back, using the hard heels of her shoes. He stifled a painful moan. *She'd just earned herself three extra stones from his catapult after church. Just wait and see.* After the praise singing, Ikem forced himself to sit through yet another sermon, taking solace in all the nasty things he would do to Uchenna after church service. Soon, Pastor Olumide's fiery threats to Satan grew fainter and fainter till…..

*****

...Ikem is perched on a log, a great gnarled log floating in a dark shimmering river. All around him is water, strewn with towering boulders and floating logs. It is night, the earth as black as the starless skies above. The air is freezing, as if Uchenna has locked him inside the giant freezer in their kitchen. He shivers and wraps his arms tightly around himself, wondering at his sudden nudity. His teeth chatter. Smoke is pouring from his mouth, as if he's lit a cigarette. Wow! *This is something he's only ever seen on telly, just like snow. He blows out air a few more times, fascinated with the denseness of the smoke he exhales.*

A dazzling brightness bursts around him, an illumination that chases away the shadows and makes black diamonds of the waters beneath his log. And in his reflection from the liquid mirror, Ikem sees that he is the light! His entire body is a blinding glow, shinning like an oblong moon in the glistening waters. Ikem gasps. He raises his arms, staring at their pulsating brightness and marvelling at the miracle of his electrifying change.

Then he hears the moans, the chilling wails that seem to rise from the depths of the murky river, filling the air, deafening him and freezing his limbs with terror. The groans...piercing, terrible...rise in intensity till Ikem is more frightened than he's ever been in his life. A long-

submerged memory suddenly surfaces, a forgotten visit to the same dark place and a terrifying encounter with...

The Blood-man!

Ikem swerves, starting to run. Except his feet aren't on the log anymore. He is suddenly weightless, light as a chicken feather...floating...rising above the log, pulled towards the solitary figure atop the massive boulder in the middle of the vast river. Oh Jesus! Egbawa o! Help! He doesn't want to go…oh Jesus please...he doesn't want to see the blood-coated man dripping blood from every pore in his coal-black body. *Ikem fights to turn away. But it is as if he's being pulled by a malignant primitive force - irresistible, relentless - to the figure of horror atop the great rock. The waters around the boulder churn violently, lashing against the blood-drenched stone, as if to claw in the keening figure above into their shadowy depths.*

Ikem shuts his eyes, his lids tight against his pupils, trying to blind himself to the bloodied horror. He tries to mouth the sign of the cross through lips frozen into silence. But all he hears are his petrified whimpers and the loud thudding of his heart. The moans from the other boulders grow in volume, pounding inside his head, swelling his bladder to breaking point. Oh Jesus! He doesn't want to wee…he doesn't want to wee! Please Jesus, don't let him wee, not now that he's no longer a cry baby…please…

Ikem grabs his groin, moaning softly, forcing his eyes to open.

Then he sees him...he sees them; the Blood-man and the Sad-men...all around the wide black river. Great boulders, each with a tall male figure atop it. Young men - strong - all in their prime, rippling muscles straining against glistening dark skin. Atop their boulders, they appear like trapped wingless birds, their arms outstretched - beseeching - asking Ikem for something he neither knows nor understands. Their moans come from a deep place beyond reach, clawing deep into Ikem's heart with a pain that brings sudden hot tears to his eyes. He chokes, his sobs tight in his throat.

'Kpele! Kpele! I'm sorry...sorry...' The words burst from his lips in a hushed whimper, a deep sorrow in his heart for their pain.

'Help us, my son! Get her to forgive us.' The voice, hollow and raspy, seems to float from Ikem's left side. It is the one place he has resolutely averted his gaze from, the boulder that terrifies him more than the rest. He forces himself to confront his nightmare, his eyes terror-wide, his body trembling with cold and fear.

And in the glow of his skin-generated light, he sees the Blood-man, the chilling spectre from his nightmare so long ago. Like the rest of the Sad-men, the Blood-man is tall and muscled. But unlike them, he is no longer in his prime. Where his eyes should have been is an empty dark hollow, dripping blood in rivulets. His entire body is a landscape of intricate small patterns, carved deep into his skin. His head is massive, his face fierce, with bushy brows framing his empty sockets. There are two feathers tucked behind each ear and thick ivory bands on his powerful arms. The ivory is blood-coated, just like the feathers. And from every opening in his body - ears, nostrils, mouth, sockets, skin - thick blood pours like an endless scarlet river, streaming down the massive boulder, coating it in red mire. Ikem feels the warm liquid break through his bladder, dampening his hands. He stares at the naked and bloody form at the peak of the great rock.

'Child of light, help us,' the Blood-man pleads, red sludge pouring from his open lips, bubbling his words, terrifying Ikem to near fainting. Yet through his terror, he sees the sadness etched into every grove in the Blood-man's face.

'I don't know what you mean,' Ikem cries, shaking his head, bewildered. 'You speak the Igbo tongue of my father's tribe but I only speak Yoruba, my mother's tongue. Your words confuse me.' He wipes his tears with the back of his hand, marvelling once again at the luminous brightness of his skin.

'You're the impossible that yet is. She will hear you; she must hear you. Please my son...get her to forgive us...forgive...'

'Forgive... forgive...'

The cries are echoed from all the other boulders, soaring through the airless night in a unified wail, filling Ikem's head, piercing his brains before plunging him into the welcome abyss of oblivion.

*****

Ikem awoke. He was lying on the hard cold floor of the church, surrounded by a sea of faces, some anxious, some curious, others suspicious. Mama's tear-streaked face was cloaked in fear and love. He felt exhausted, weak, as if he'd done none-stop PE at school for over a month.

'Praise the Lord! Alleluia! He's awake!' Pastor's thick bible flashed across Ikem's face as Mama stooped to press him into her great bosom. He burrowed into her folds, needing her shelter and warmth. His heart was still pounding from a lingering terror that had followed him across the boundaries of dreamland to the real world. He desperately wanted to protect himself with the sign of the cross but that would require him leaving the safety of

Mama's arms. Ikem felt a wetness in his trousers and groaned in silent shame. *Oh Jesus! Oluwa o! He had wet himself like a cry-baby...in front of everyone too. His friends would never play with him again...everyone has seen his shame...*

He started to cry, his body shuddering against Mama's chest.

'Ike boy! My son, what's the matter? What happened? Tell me.' Mama's anxious voice broke into his humiliation, steering his mind back to the fear, the darkness, the sorrow...*and the light*. Ikem lifted his head, raising his hands to his gaze. No light...no glow. Just ordinary hands, free of magic and glory. *But he had glowed!* Back in that sad place of darkness, he had glowed! The Blood-man had called him child of light. He wanted *her* to forgive them.

'The Blood-man said I must ask her to forgive them,' Ikem's voice was urgent, insistent. 'They're all so sad, Mama...and it's very dark and the river is black and they're all crying because she won't forgive them but the Blood-man said I'm the child of light and she will hear me...she...'

He broke off as he heard the loud gasps from the congregation. He saw Pastor's stunned face and the bewilderment in Mama's eyes.

'Ikem! Ike boy! What are you talking about, my son?' Mama was shaking him, fear cloaking her plump face. 'Who is this Blood-man you talk about and who is the woman who won't forgive him? Where did you meet this Blood-man? Uchenna! You wicked girl! Where have you taken my son in my absence? Tell me now, you wretched girl. Who is this Blood-man and where does he live? Talk girl! Talk before I break your skull.'

Ikem felt his head hit the hard floor of the church as Mama rushed at Uchenna, who was cowering behind some of the parishioners, eyes wide with terror. For a fleeting second, he felt pleasure at witnessing Uchenna's fear but that joy disappeared as quickly as it came.

'Mama!' He clutched her blue lace *Buba* kaftan. 'Mama, it's not Uchenna. She didn't take me anywhere.' He felt all eyes once more on him and wished he could fly away, the way he had flown in his dream…*dream?* He drew his knees close, unwilling to expose the damp evidence of his shame to the curious crowd.

'The boy is possessed!' Pastor suddenly shouted, raising his bible high in the air. There were shocked gasps and murmurs. Words like "Asmodius", "witchcraft" and "demons" ricocheted around the church, bringing a sudden sharp pain to Ikem's head. He shut his eyes, trying to shut out the pain, wanting nothing more than his bed and a change of trousers and a bowl of Sunday rice. But already, Pastor's hand was on Ikem's head, his fingers digging painfully into his scalp as if strangling the devil lurking inside his mind. The loud shouts of the prayer warriors intensified his headache as they proceeded to caste out the demons and "principalities" from him. There were fevered chants of "Alleluia" and "Praise the Lord" from the congregation; even Mama joined.

Ikem had no idea how long he lay on the church floor, soaked in his own shameful piss till his torture ended with another drenching; this time with holy water from Pastor's sanctified armoury, splashed liberally over his head, Jesus-guaranteed to annihilate Satan and his minions. He shivered, waiting for a sign that would show him that he was finally free of possession, though he couldn't recall when exactly Satan had taken possession of his soul, apart from stupidly falling asleep in church and having a nightmare.

Yet, as they drove home in Mama's car, Ikem knew that the devil-thrashing holy water had failed to destroy his memory of the Blood-man and the Sad-men. S*urely, it was just a dream...just a horrible dream...and dreams are not real...especially when dreamt in a holy place like a church. Teach him to fall asleep in Jesus' house in future! Never, ever again.*

*****

A few weeks after his thirteenth birthday, Ikem's father decided to relocate the family back to his home town, Enugu, located in the Eastern part of Nigeria, formerly known as the Republic of Biafra. Mama didn't want to leave Lagos and her family for the hilly coal-mining city of Enugu. Ikem didn't want to settle in Enugu either. Like Mama, he couldn't speak the Igbo language of the East and worried about fitting in. But Papa's mother was very sick and Papa wanted to be near her. Like Ikem, Papa was an only child and being a doctor, felt it was his duty to take care of his mother in her old age. That was the explanation he'd given when Ikem kicked up a fuss about the planned move.

Ikem had met his paternal grandmother a few times and felt neither affection nor dislike for her. From snippets of gossip he'd picked up from Uchenna, he knew his grandmother didn't like Mama much because Mama was from a different tribe. It was all rather baffling to him, since he knew his mother had Igbo blood in her ancestry. Grandmama Modupe, his maternal grandmother, had told him several times how her great, great, great-grandmother had been an Igbo woman. No one could remember what village she came from. It had all been such a long time ago.

But the fact remained that Mama was not hundred percent Yoruba, something that should have pleased his Enugu grandmother. Because of her, he now faced the horrid prospect of leaving his school, his friends and his Lagos cousins forever.

The night before their departure, Ikem was carried back to the water-place of eternal darkness and wailing Sad-men.

*****

He feels again the freezing stagnant air. This time, a foul odour permeates the air, making him gag. It is a stench of rotten fish and decayed meat...and fear. He smells the fear in the ominous silence like a tangible and solid thing.

The fearsome wailing of a damned soul rips the air. It comes from somewhere towards his left. In seconds, the entire place is filled with the keening of the Sad-men, their groans all encompassing, overwhelming and awful. Ikem clasps his ears with his hands. His heart fills with dread and the familiar sorrow he's experienced on his previous encounters with the Blood-man. His skin breaks out in goosebumps and he shivers with a cold that seeps through to his bone marrow. In the dark waters, thick smoke rises in dense swirls, stinging his eyes. And as before, his body is a kaleidoscope of lights, shimmering…glowing.

This time, his light struggles to slice through the dense mist, its glow pathetic and almost powerless against the cloudy darkness of the water-hell. He feels himself becoming weightless as before. He is floating upwards… forward, sideways… flitting high into the air with little control over his flight. In the dim glow of his light, he sees them as before, the Sad-men, trapped on their individual boulders, wailing into the night. This time, they are not standing upright and strong. Each Sad-man crouches in an identical posture, shoulders hunched, heads bowed into their knees and arms clasped over their heads. None of them look up at Ikem as he calls out to them and their rejection terrifies him even more than their howls.

He feels that magnetic pull again, the irresistible force that draws him towards the one boulder he dreads the most. Gripped with fear, he fights to hold back - to resist - to escape. But it is like fighting a playground tug-of-war with the boys from the senior classes. Ikem finds himself in front of the Blood-man, his feet hovering just a few inches from the great blood-soaked boulder. The rock pulses with malignant awareness, like a living presence…an evil entity. It scares the breath out of his lungs. Ikem is held, locked in his fear, as unresisting as a mesmerised prey awaiting its death. The Blood-man oozes more blood than ever. The thick dark-red fluid pours in an endless pool from his entire body, matting his hair and caking his face with its awful sludge. How can so much blood pour from one single man? Ikem wonders, his eyes wide with terror.

Unlike the Sad-men, the Blood-man stands upright on his rocky prison, the black holes of his sockets staring sightlessly into the dark skies. His aged face wears a hopeless look that brings a lump to Ikem's throat. It is the same look he sometimes catches on Papa's face when Papa doesn't know anyone is around - only worse... much worse. In a heart-beat, the Blood-man fixes his sightless gaze at Ikem, his bloody visage sending a chill through his body. Ikem's head spins and he thinks he will pass out.

'Child of light, the impossible that yet is; Hurry! Find her before it is too late. She is even now, poised to strike down another of my bloodline. How long will her fury last? How long must we suffer? Go, blessed traveller of the worlds. Keep my son away from Etiti, for there lies his doom and my curse. Hurry! Hurry!'

Then the Blood-man does what all the Sad-men have done and bows his head to his knees, howling into the black river in anguished hopelessness.

Ikem flees...

*****

...Right back to his twitching body on the thin mattress in his furniture-stripped bedroom. As his eyes opened, he heard his breath, harsh and loud in the dark room. He felt the cold wetness of sweat on his body. *Oluwa o! Jesus!* His heart was racing and his mouth was dry. Without crossing himself with the customary sign of the cross, he dashed over to the light switch by the door and flooded his room with a welcome brightness that temporarily chased away the horrors of his nightmare.

Except this time, he knew it wasn't a nightmare anymore...had never been a nightmare...only he'd been too stupid to understand, block-head that he was. But now, he knew...*he knew*...knew that the Blood-man and the Sad-men were real. The water-hell of endless night was a real place; and he, Ikem Ani, had become a night-flyer, one of the reviled *Amosu* night-flyers that Uchenna used to frighten him with in his younger years. Hadn't the Blood-man called him "blessed traveller of the worlds"? Except he wasn't blessed. He was cursed; cursed to leave his body and be drawn into the world of the undead, into the dreams of the living and into the unknown realms of the universe like a moth to flame. There was nothing he could do about it...*nothing. When had he been bitten by an Amosu? Who amongst his friends was an Amosu? Kunle? No...Kunle's parents were born-again Christians. Maybe Biodun... perhaps not. Biodun could swim very well and Amosu demons were afraid of water.*

Uchenna! That was it! It had to be Uchenna…it was always someone you trusted that ended up biting the dreaded *Amosu* virus into your blood. *Oluwa o!* What would be his fate if anyone ever found out he had become a night-flyer? Worse, Uchenna had gone back to her people when Papa decided they were relocating to Enugu. No wonder she'd been happy to leave Lagos, knowing what she had done. In order to rid himself of the evil, he would need to find her and bite her back, returning her curse to her. But then, Mama would be suspicious if he started asking about Uchenna's whereabouts.

Ikem sat on the thin mattress, his brain sifting through his dream-memory. What was it the Blood-man had said? Something about his son going to Enugu… no…Etim…he knew it started with an "E" but he couldn't for the life of him remember the name. And who was his son anyway? How was Ikem supposed to find this son and tell him not to go to the place that would be his doom? And the evil woman that would not forgive them…who was she? How was he supposed to find her even if he wanted to…which he didn't? Ikem shook his head. The whole business terrified the wits out of him and he wished never to return to that accursed place with its wailing men. In a way, it was a good thing Papa was taking them back to Enugu. He knew Uchenna came from somewhere near the place. Maybe he could find a way to trace her village and give her back her curse. *Jesus!* How he hated that evil girl. He had never trusted her and now he knew he had good cause for his distrust. To be stuck for life with this evil *Amosu* infection was more than he could bear to think about.

*****

The day after their arrival at their new home in Enugu, a three-bedroom bungalow with a large compound and a grove of mango trees, Papa announced that the family would be driving up the infamous Milliken Hill to visit Ikem's grandmother at her village. Papa told Ikem that the mountainous road was named after the white colonial engineer who had supervised its construction, Mr Milliken. Lots of people from Papa's village had died during the construction of that road, making it the most notorious road in that part of Nigeria. He couldn't wait to see the road;

something to text his friends in Lagos about and maybe post on his Facebook page.

When Papa mentioned his grandmother's village, a wave of terror shot through Ikem, almost sending him fleeing in panic. *Etiti!* Papa's mother lived at Etiti, the place he had tried in vain to recollect, the very village the Blood-man had said his son must never visit! *But who was his son? Surely he couldn't have been referring to Papa.* Ikem knew the Blood-man wasn't his grandfather. He had seen pictures of Papa's father who had died in a stabbing attack when Papa was a young boy. The Blood-man didn't look anything like the picture he'd seen and with the new insight he now had about his *Amosu* condition, Ikem knew without the slightest doubt that the Blood-man was a ghost; same as the Sad-men; all restless spirits, trapped in a dark watery hell he had no name for. Which still left the question - who was the Blood-man's son and how was he to find the man and warn him about Etiti, even if he was fool enough to say any such thing anyway?

Ikem still remembered his terrible ordeal in the church after his second encounter with the Blood-man; how Pastor had branded him possessed by Asmodius and Principalities; the suspicious looks on the faces of the parishioners at his potential demon possession; Mama's terror, Uchenna's subsequent teasing… No; he didn't want to be branded demon possessed ever again. Nor did he want his terrible secret exposed. To be exposed as a night-flyer meant to be ostracised and reviled. *Chei! Oluwa o!* What he wouldn't do to see that evil girl, Uchenna, dead.

Later that morning, as Ikem wandered around the new house, familiarising himself with the place, he pondered over something his Lagos Grandmama Modupe had told him before they left Lagos.

'My child, listen to your heart when you arrive in Enugu,' she'd said. 'Remember, towns are just like people. They either accept you or reject you. Some towns are like prostitutes, especially tourist towns. Those places will accept anyone who has money to spend on them. But just know that most towns will let you know whether or not they accept you. Just listen to your heart and follow your senses. If you know you're not welcome in Enugu, tell your mother immediately and she will bring you straight back to Lagos, okay?'

Ikem had listened to his grandmother without really understanding what she meant. *How can a town tell you it doesn't like you?* He'd left his grandmother and hurried over to his cousins to say goodbye. Now, twenty-four hours after arriving in Enugu, he found himself recalling his grandmother's words with some unease. He didn't like Enugu and something told him that Enugu didn't want him either. There was a *wrongness* in the air - a tense waiting, unseen eyes full of malevolence, watching him…waiting…

Ikem shivered, glancing nervously over his shoulders. He would give it a few weeks before asking Mama to send him back to Grandmama Modupe in Lagos.

Later, as he wandered back to his room, he overheard his parents engaged in a muted, yet, intense discussion. He'd never been one to eavesdrop on his parents but there was something about Papa's voice that drew him to their bedroom door, an underlying emotion he could only describe as unease…fear. He'd never known his proud father to exhibit any trace of fear in all his life. As a doctor, Papa had seen all kinds of terrible things, even lots of dead people. Yet, something…someone had managed to infuse his father's blood with terror.

'I have no words to describe the woman,' Ikem heard Papa say, his voice barely audible through the slight gap of their bedroom door. 'Truth be told, I can't even call her a woman in any sense of the word. Just remembering her face makes me shudder. Never have I seen such ugliness…such evil and hatred on a person's face. And her laugh…God have mercy! The sound of that terrible cackle still rings in my ears even now. I've been asking myself why on earth I should have such a horrible dream. You know me, Yinka. I'm not one to dream or lay any store by them. But I tell you, this dream has affected me in a way I can't even begin to describe.' As Papa paused, Ikem pressed his ears closer to the door, his heart thudding wildly. *A dream! Another awful nightmare; except this time, it was Papa having it.*

'I told you we should have got a Pastor to consecrate this house before we moved into it but you wouldn't listen.' Mama's voice was a mixture of exasperation and anxiety. 'That's the problem with you, Ezeoha. You just never listen to anything concerning church. You don't know the kind of people that lived in this house before we moved in. For all we know, they might have been witches, devil-worshippers or even people that consult witchdoctors or use juju. Don't shake your head, Ezeoha. Just listen to me. You don't know everything as you believe you do. All I'm saying is that you might have picked up the residues of their evil in your dreams. And whether you like it or not, as soon as we finish visiting your mother, I'll arrange for a pastor to come and pray over the house and consecrate it with holy water. I know you have no belief in pastors but this time just humour me, ok?'

Ikem quickly crept off to his room, careful to mute his footsteps. There was a feeling of anxiety, none-the-less tinged with relief at knowing he wasn't the only one having nightmares, even though he now suspected his nightmares were more than mere dreams. Maybe Papa might decide to take them back to Lagos if his bad dreams continued. Perhaps Papa's nightmare was Enugu's way of telling them it didn't want them, just as Grandmama Modupe had warned.

Later in the day as they drove up the winding and pot-holed asphalt of the infamous Milliken Hill, Ikem tried to push aside his unease. Papa's face wore that sad look he'd witnessed on a few occasions. Ikem had always wondered what put such sorrow in Papa's face. But he'd never dared ask because Papa would know he'd seen him. He figured it had something to do with the fact that they couldn't have any more kids after him. Papa probably got teased by his friends the way Ikem's friends teased him about being an only child. They said he was the one eye that owed an eternal debt to the blind man. The slightest trouble would result in total blindness - his death; no Ikem, no more kids for his parents, their family name lost for eternity.

Ikem tried to concentrate on the games on his mobile phone. Apart from his fear of Etiti, there was something about the steep and narrow road snaking up the dark and ominous Milliken Hill that sent his heart racing in a bad way. Initially, he'd started off taking pictures of the wild landscape, the hulking face of the hill and great hanging trees; pictures he planned to post on his Facebook page. But as the journey progressed, Facebook and his friends became the last things on his mind. Each time they turned a sharp curve, Ikem shut his eyes tight, petrified by the yawning deep precipice at their side of the road. It appeared like a bottomless ravine, landscaped with dwarf trees and wild shrub. He'd never realised he had a fear of heights till they drove up the awful Milliken Hill. Papa kept cursing the reckless drivers that took the curves at speeds unsuited to the narrow road. From his seat at the back of the car, Ikem felt his heart skip each time a car drove down the opposite direction, praying for the journey to end.

Suddenly, he heard Papa shout, slamming the brakes with a violence that flung Ikem forward, banging his head on the front headrest. The car shuddered to a sudden stop right in the middle of the road.

'Ezeoha! Jesus! What is it?' Mama screamed, her voice shrill and deafening in the small confines of their 505 Peugeot car. Papa just shook his head, pointing a trembling finger to the front of their car. Ikem could see beads of perspiration on Papa's forehead despite the cool blast of the air conditioning in the car. His face wore a terrible fear that sent the chill down Ikem's spine.

'Ezeoha, speak to me,' shouted Mama, shaking Papa's shoulder with fear-induced violence. 'What are you pointing at? I can't see anything.'

Neither could Ikem, try as he could to follow the direction of Papa's pointing hand. Already, cars were blaring their horns impatiently behind them, demanding an instant end to the unnecessary bottle-neck. Ikem felt an acute embarrassment that almost chased his fears away.

'It's her…' Papa finally stuttered, his voice hushed, steeped in terror.

'Who? Who?' Mama screamed.

'Her…the hag…from my dream…there, in front of the car. Oh my God! I can't bear to look at her face…' Papa's voice whimpered into a low moan. Ikem felt his blood run cold. *Her! How was it possible to see your dreams in real life?* But Papa wasn't one to imagine things and grown-ups didn't play silly tricks for no reason.

'Papa, let's go back home now…please,' Ikem's voice was as urgent as the blaring horns behind. There was a loud voice screaming silently inside his head, *"Get away from here! Get away from Enugu...now!"* 'Please Papa, let's just go home now. We can visit grandmother another day.' Ikem's hand was hard on Papa's shoulder, pressing home his request. Papa shook his head, wiping the sweat off his face with the back of his hand.

'It's okay, my son,' Papa said, forcing a smile to his face, his voice strained, like one nursing a cold. 'It's nothing. I think maybe I had too little sleep last night, what with the long drive from Lagos yesterday and the unpacking. But everything's fine now. We'll be in Etiti in no time and I'm sure your grandmother and cousins will be excited to see you again after all these years.' Mama's smile tried to echo the reassurance in Papa's words but Ikem could still see the terror lurking beneath the brown pupils of her eyes.

Soon, the car was in motion again as they began to inch up the narrow road. Papa was driving so slowly that he soon caused a long queue of cars behind. Their impatient horns kept urging them forward till Papa gave in and picked up speed once again. It was as if he was suddenly in a hurry to get away from Milliken Hill and whatever horror he had seen on that dark road. Ikem looked behind and saw that a welcome gap had developed between them and the cars behind and the sight pleased him. He returned his attention to the game on his mobile. Papa turned on the car radio, tuning into a noisy station playing some gospel music by a local singer with a shrill voice that jarred rather than soothed the senses. Ikem frowned, irritated. He pulled out his earphones from his shirt pocket, intent on plugging out the irritating song.

He was in the process of pushing in the second plug into his left ear when he heard Papa's shout, coupled with Mama's scream. The car began to swerve in a violent criss-cross over the road.

'It's her! It's her, oh my God in heaven! She won't get out of the road…oh God…oh God!' Papa's shouts were swallowed by Mama's terrified screams and Ikem felt something warm and wet dampen his trousers as the car became airborne, falling, somersaulting, rolling, bumping…screams, a sharp pain, terror…darkness. And then, all was still.

*****

He is walking along a dusty path, the earth, sun-baked to hard red clay. On both sides of the path are stunted trees and wild foliage. A few cassava farms add to the greenery of the landscape, their mounds surrounded with spinach and Onugbu *bitter-leaf plants. Ikem is not alone. Mama is holding his hand and her face wears a harried and hurried look.* But where is Papa? *Ikem looks over his shoulders but all he sees are trees and the funny little houses made of mud and thatched roofs, as round as the cassava mounds along the dusty path. He recalls seeing similar houses in some Nollywood films he'd watched in Lagos. Now he knows they're real and not some made-up film setting.*

Mama keeps pulling him forward, her steps urgent, her face, tight. Her flowered wrapper billows around her in the gentle breeze and beads of moisture dots her forehead beneath her permed fringe. All around them are sounds; birds' tweets, grasshoppers' chirps, children's laughter, women's voices, barking dogs and bleating goats. A small grey lizard darts across their path, closely pursued by a bigger lizard with a red crest. They pause and stare at Ikem, nodding their heads as if in greeting before darting off to the nearest tree. Ikem smiles, fascinated. The air smells of smoke, dust and cooking, reminding him he's very hungry…ravenous…and thirsty. The overhead noonday sun is merciless in its intensity and his shirt is already soaked with sweat. But Mama is in a great hurry and soon, he finds himself inside a hamlet just off the dry clay path.

He looks around in wonder. There are lots of those funny red mud huts dotted around the hamlet in a circular position. He counts nine huts altogether. The place is crowded with people, mostly women and children. They are all in a state of near-nudity, save for some flimsy cloth around their hips. The women's skins are covered in intricate leopard paw prints, their eye-lids lined with dark Uli *eye-paint. A group of little girls are playing the popular clap and dance* Oga *game while the boys chase grasshoppers and each other. Their voices fill the air with near-festive joy. Goats, dogs and chickens mill around the flat sandy ground of the hamlet, unfazed by their human masters. A strong smell of burning and cooked food permeates the air, bringing a cosy warmth to Ikem's heart.*

He notices a towering and wide-branched Iroko tree which dominates the compound like a hunched monster. It is situated at the centre of the hamlet, its broad branches casting dark shadows beneath it. For a second, he considers taking shelter from the blazing sun beneath its cool shade but then he sees what lies at the base of the great tree.

Around the exposed thick roots of the tree are several calabashes and pots, some empty, others, loaded with food in various stages of decomposition. There are live chickens tied to the roots, as well as dead poultry. He sees feathers everywhere, some white, others black and brown, all blood-splattered. Some feathers stick to the pots while others attach themselves to the tree trunk like flies to cattle. There is an aura of death....of immense power...around the Iroko tree, as if a cold presence observes the hamlet and its people from the leafy eyes of the great tree. Ikem shivers and draws himself closer to Mama. The last thing he wants is to make any contact with the shrine tree. Mama pauses. She looks around, as if in search of something...someone.

A woman emerges from one of the huts, the smallest hut in the hamlet, closely followed by a young girl. He thinks the girl might be the same age as himself or maybe a year older - fourteen years at the most. Her exposed breasts are small and pointy. Ikem looks away in embarrassment. As the older woman turns her face to their direction, Mama gasps. Ikem also stares in amazement, tightening his grip on Mama's hand. For the woman with the young girl is none other than Mama, his own mother! Oluwa o! *What is going on? Does Mama have a twin sister? What is her twin sister doing in this strange place? Why is everyone naked?*

As he continues to stare, he notices subtle differences between Mama and her twin. The woman is naked and her hair is short and kinky, unlike Mama's sleek Perm. Her naked body is slimmer than Mama's round curves and her skin is covered in intricate leopard paw designs drawn in thick black ink. Her nose is slightly broader than Mama's nose. The unmarked skin of her face is a lighter shade of brown than Mama's darker hue. Otherwise, one could easily mistake her for his mother.

Mama's twin hugs the young girl close to her as they walk towards another hut in the hamlet. This hut is separated from the rest by a wooden fence. It is also the largest hut in the hamlet, being the size of three huts put together. Mama pulls Ikem along as she hurries after her twin and the young girl. He wonders why nobody speaks to them or even acknowledges their presence; not the numerous children fighting and playing or the women cooking in various open fires. He sees another woman standing inside what appears to be a hollowed tree trunk filled with palm kennels. She is mashing the nuts with her feet, which are as red as the red palm oil she extracts from the nuts. Some children are standing by the thick log begging to be allowed into the oily swill. They pester and cry till the woman finally lets them in. Soon, their happy squeals fill the air and Ikem looks on, a sad yearning in his heart. They seem to be having fun, which is more than he can say for himself. Again, he is struck by the distinct absence of men in the hamlet. He remembers Papa. Where on earth is Papa?

A thought seeps through his mind, a sadness, a recollection of something unpleasant...frightening. But it disappears as quickly as it comes and he quickens his steps to Mama's own. Soon, they are standing right outside the large hut, watching Mama's twin and the young girl disappear inside. After a moment's hesitation, Mama follows them in, stooping to avoid contact with the door's dry wood frame. He finds himself in a wide circular hall, cool and dark despite the blazing midday sun outside. The room smells of stale sweat, palm-wine and tobacco snuff.

As his eyes adapt to the gloom, Ikem sees other people in the hall. He counts ten men in total, seven of them seated on what appears to be wooden stools, their backs turned to the dwarf door of the hut. The men on the stool are naked to the waist, their loin cloth covering their lower back. There are feathers perched on both sides of their ears and intricate designs carved into their skin. Unlike the markings on the womenfolk which are done with black ink, the men's are carved into their skin with sharp blades, deep and eternal.

*As Ikem sees the body marks, something cold settles in his spine like icy fingers. He knows those body marks! He has seen them somewhere….*somewhere. *One of the seated men, the one wearing an ivory band on his arm, turns round and Ikem gasps, staring wide-eyed at the familiar fierce face.*

The Blood-man!

Except his eyes are no longer dark hollow pits, but piercing black orbs framed by bushy brows. His body is still as powerful as Ikem remembers, muscular like the body of a warrior. The man seated closest to the Blood-man, on the right-hand side, turns around and Ikem sees a younger miniature of the Blood-man. He knows instinctively that he is looking at a father and son.

The other three men standing are different from the Blood-man, both in stature and clothing. For one thing, they are partially clothed, their legs covered by loose trousers tied to their waist with cords. Their bare chests are free of skin carvings and they carry skin bags slung low across their shoulders. One of the men carries what looks like a long rifle and appears to be the leader of the standing men. Ikem notices that he has three deep lines cut into both sides of his cheeks and when he speaks to his companions, Ikem instantly recognises the tongue – Yoruba, the language of Mama's people. Hearing the familiar Lagos tongue fills his heart with warmth, chasing away his anxiety.

As Mama's twin draws further into the hall, the Blood-man gives an imperceptible nod to the three standing men. With a rush of bodies, they grab the young girl and wrestle her to the hard mud flooring of the hut. As Ikem stares in stunned disbelief, the men quickly bind her arms and legs with a thick rope, paying scant heed to her screams and tears. The seated men look on impassively, doing nothing to assist the child.

'Nne! Nne! Help me, Nne!' The child cries, her head turned in desperate terror to her mother, Mama's

twin. The mother rushes to her young daughter with a loud wail. But the Blood-man and his son pull her back, knocking her down to the floor and pinning her down with their arms. Their cruel fists rain blows on her face, which is soon bloodied and swollen. The seated men look away, feigning invisibility. Mama rushes forward and Ikem joins her, shame and anger spurring his attack on the Blood-man and his evil son. But he is beating at thin air, his fists going through their bodies as if through water, harmless and useless. He feels tears of fury dampen his face as Mama rushes over to assist the trapped child. But her blows are as ineffective as his and soon, she too is sobbing in helpless frustration. Mama's twin is still on the floor, screaming, pleading.

'Ezeoha! What have we done to you that you inflict this evil on us?' She wails at the Blood-man, her tears flowing like an endless stream. 'Haven't we suffered enough at your hands? Please, I beg you, spare my only child. In the name of all our gods and ancestors, I beseech you. Do not sell my only child to these people-hunters from the water-lands. You have other children from your other wives. You have other family members you can trade. I have nothing...nothing...except my Ndidi. She's my life, the only reason I have carried on living in the harsh hardship of your hamlet. I am an object of mockery among your

other wives and the entire people of Etiti. I have no son to defend my honour or secure my place in your hamlet; only my child, Ndidi…this sweet child the gods have used to wipe my tears. Please my husband, do not sell her to these evil men. You know we are not river people. We cannot swim. Don't let them take my only child down the river to the white men, please. Sell me instead but spare my child. I am worthless to you. I can't give you a son and my womb has soured. Sell me… please…'

Etiti! So that's where they are, *Ikem thinks. Suddenly, he feels himself recoil as the Blood-man knocks the words out of Mama's twin, kicking the prostrate woman with his bare feet. His son joins him in the attack and yet again, Ikem rushes forward to fight them, even as he knows the futility of his actions. The child continues to cry out piteously to her mother till the slave traders bundle her up into a big raffia bag on the floor. They hand a bulging bag to the Blood-man, shake hands with both father and son and quickly exit the hut with their human cargo.*

As they leave, Mama's twin lets out a piercing scream and rises to give chase. But once again, she is restrained by the Blood-man and his son, who rain more blows on her body. Mama is shouting at them, cursing them, trying to protect her twin. But her voice is as invisible as her presence. Ikem feels a burning hatred for the Blood-man, an intense loathing that leaves him shaking with rage. After witnessing his brutality to his wife and daughter, he is glad...very glad...that the Blood-man is now suffering in that dark water-hell of his nightmares.

A silence descends in the hut as the abused woman on the floor falls into a stupor. The Blood-man and his son exchange anxious looks. The other clansmen on the stools rise to investigate. They stoop and lift the woman's lids. Her eyes roll. She lives. They exchange cruel smiles and abandon her. They gather in a circle on the hard floor and empty the contents of the big bag left by the slave-traders. Brass or copper bands spill out of the bag, lots of them. The men gasp in admiration as the Blood-man counts the bands - fifty in total. They nod in satisfaction, their faces wreathed in smiles.

'Fifty Okpohos. We have done well with this sale. It should re-thatch my hut. Obinna, give two Okpohos to each kinsman and tie up the rest for me,' the Blood-man instructs his son.

A movement draws Ikem's attention. The prone woman on the floor rises to her knees. Her eyes are swollen and bloodshot. Her lips are bruised and her nose is broken. Her entire face is a glistening gore of blood, tears and sweat. She crawls towards her husband and his clansmen, her nose leaking blood, which leaves dark stains on the earthen floor.

'Murderers! Thieves! Shameless cowards! I curse you and your sons to eternity,' she screams pointing an accusing finger at them. 'As you have taken my daughter away, so shall your sons, their sons and their sons' sons be taken from this day hence. Hear me, Ezeoha Ani! No sons born to you shall live to see the full years allocated to them by the gods. They will die in their prime, violent and sudden deaths. Your house shall be a desolate place and your name, a cursed one. Mark my words all you evil cowards. I curse you and your house to....'

Ikem looks on in horror as the Blood-man and his son cut the words from the deranged mother, smashing her head into the hard floor of the hut. The blood gushes freely from her crushed skull, flowing towards the shiny brass bands still on the floor. The Blood-man rushes to gather them away but he is not fast enough. Some of the bands are now dual-coloured - yellow and red. The sight twists something in Ikem's heart. Blood money, *he thinks;* cursed money. *The Blood-man and his kinsmen stare at the still woman on the floor. This time, they do not bother to lift her lids. They know that she is dead; and they want her dead. She is the final witness to their dastardly deed and her death buries their crime for eternity.*

Mama is sobbing bitterly as she leads him away from the murder scene and Ikem struggles to stem his own tears. For now he knows who the Blood-man is. Mama's twin had called him Ezeoha Ani, the same name Papa bears. The Blood-man is his ancestor, his great, great, great-grandfather - he isn't sure how many "greats" but they must be many. Papa is therefore the son that must never visit Etiti and now Ikem knows why.

'We have to find Papa now,' he says to Mama, his voice urgent, his steps hurried. 'We can't let him come to Etiti to see his mother or he will die. Hurry Mama; hurry...hurry...

*****

Ikem woke up in a small room with white-washed walls and a sluggish overhead fan. His head was throbbing and his body felt as if he had fallen off a hundred bicycles in quick succession. He noticed that his right arm was in a white cast, the same as both his legs. When he raised his undamaged left arm to his head, his hand met the coarse fabric of a bandage. By his bedside, a half-empty bag of saline drip hung on a metal stand, its long white tube attached to his arm. The smell of disinfectant was strong in the room and his eyes felt heavy, as if weighted down with rocks. He tried to get his bearing, willing his mind to recall his hazy memory. He was in a hospital of some kind; that much was clear to him. But why was he in a hospital and where were his parents? He tried to call out to someone, a nurse, a doctor…anyone. But his throat felt raw and the words stuck in his lungs.

Then, he remembered! It all came back with water clarity. *He had been at Etiti with Mama!* He had witnessed the Blood-man and his kinsmen murder Mama's twin sister after selling her only child to the Yoruba slave-traders. Except it wasn't really Mama's twin sister. It couldn't be because it had all happened such a long time ago when the Blood-man was still young and people went around in the nude. So who was the woman then? She had to be related to Mama somehow. The resemblance was too striking to be coincidental. And where was Mama anyway? He needed to find her to discuss the events they had witnessed together.

Ikem felt a sudden unease that had little to do with his injuries. There was something he wasn't remembering…something urgent…something that needed to be done in a hurry. But his mind was too fuzzy and his head too painful to remember. Hot tears spilled from his eyes, hard sobs hurting his chest, making his pains almost unbearable. A woozy feeling was drowning his head and an indescribable weight was crushing his chest. He tried to call out for help but there was no breath left in his lungs. *Mama....Papa...Mama...* He wasn't sure if he spoke out the words, if anyone heard his voice. *Oh Jesus! Please Jesus!* He didn't want to die alone. *He didn't want to die.* He felt himself falling into a deep abyss, a frightening dark place he did not want to see. He tried to fight it, to resist its pull. But he was too weak and the darkness too strong. And finally, with a low moan, he gave in to the black void.

*****

He is looking into the face of a man lying underneath a palm-tree, a young man he instantly recognises as the son of the Blood-man. It is the same son that had assisted in the selling of his own sister and the murder of his stepmother. Obinna. *That is the name the Blood-man had called him that evil afternoon of betrayal and murder. But the young man is now dead, his eyes staring vacantly at the bent fronds of the palm-tree above. His head is a bloody pulp and white blood-spattered matter ooze out of his smashed skull. Not far from the dead man are a broken rope and a smashed gourde. Ikem smells, even before he sees the damp soil by the gourde.* Palm-wine. *He guesses Obinna must have fallen from the palm-tree while tapping for palm-wine. He glances up at the tree. It is a very long fall.*

By the side of the dead youth is the Blood-man. His face is a picture of shock and anguish as he stares at the bloody corpse of his first son and heir. He is holding his dead boy, rocking, moaning. His eyes are swollen and bloodshot. His body is covered in brown dust and sweat. Ikem hears the women of the hamlet wailing, pulling their hair. The men beat their chests in anger at the senseless death of a young man in the prime of his life.

*In the midst of the keening, he hears a sound that sends the cold chill of pure terror down his spine. He hears the gleeful cackle of a female, high-pitched and triumphant. It is coming somewhere overhead, atop the palm-tree. He lifts his head to the tree and his heart almost stops. His skin breaks out in terror-bumps. Cold sweat dampens his body and he struggles to breath. He is trembling so violently he fears he will collapse in a faint. He wants to faint...*oh Jesus! *He wants to faint so he doesn't see the horror above the palm-tree.*

Perched on the lowest frond like a bird of prey is Mama's twin, her face as bloodied and broken as it had been the day the Blood-man murdered her. But death has given her a visage that is as appalling as it is truly terrible. Her skin is an ashy hue, her barred teeth, sharp and pointy beneath blood-coated lips. Death has lengthened her hair into wild knots which fail to cover the deep bloody gash in her head. Hard talon-tipped hands grasp the branches like eagle claws, shaking the fronds with manic glee. Her thighs are spread wide, obscene and terrible. Bloody piss gushes from her body, drenching the corpse underneath the palm-tree.

Without warning, her blood-shot gaze zeroes into his eyes. They are piercing, fierce and furious. Ikem gasps, stumbling back and falling on his buttocks. He feels the sharp sting of pain as he bruises his palm on the rough sandy soil. His heart thuds so wildly he thinks he will die. Oh Jesus! Oluwa o! *He has seen a ghost…real ghost…and she has seen him too!* Jesus! Egbawa o! Help! *Where is Mama? Where is Papa?*

He hears a sudden shout and sees the Blood-man on his feet, stumbling backwards, away from his son's corpse. He is pointing to the top of the Palm-tree, his eyes terror-wide. His body is trembling as violently as the palm fronds overhead.

'It's her! Oh my ancestors save me! It's her!' The Blood-man is almost incoherent as he struggles to free himself from his kinsmen. They follow his pointing finger but see nothing save for the waving fronds thrashing violently in the still noon-day air. They find nothing amiss

in the strange behaviour of the fronds. The tree has taken the life of the boy after all. It is only normal that nature should weep for the untimely death of a strong young man.

They try to drag the Blood-man away from the tragic scene, urging him to take heart, to be a man and not allow himself to be overwhelmed by grief. The Blood-man doesn't resist. He is suddenly drained by terror, his massive frame, a shivering lump. But even as they draw him away, Ikem hears the terrible and malicious cackle follow them, mocking the Blood-man.

'This is only the beginning, Ezeoha Ani,' she screeches, her voice a piercing hollowness that reverberates in his head. 'I told you your house will be barren of sons for all eternity. Be prepared dear husband. For you shall yet meet me again as you dig another grave for another of your precious sons. Their blood shall be on your head alone, for you have sealed their doom with your evil. Go and bury your first son but make sure you dig enough graves for your other sons and their sons' sons.' With another loud cackle, the ghost vanishes, leaving Ikem as stunned and petrified as the Blood-man.

Oh Jesus! *He finally knows who she is; she who will not forgive, she who has condemned the Blood-man and the Sad-men to their dark purgatory in the water land! And the Blood-man is foolish enough to wonder how long her fury will last, to ask him to beg her forgiveness after all he'd done to her?*

Ikem turns to flee. He must escape before she changes her mind and kills him. He must find Papa quickly before she kills him too. He has to find Mama and get her to stop Papa going to Etiti. He must hurry...hurry...

*****

'Hurry! Get adrenaline! We're losing him,' Ikem thought he heard those words as a burning pain in his chest yanked him up from his bed before sending him crashing back again. Waves of agony spread right through his body. He heard many voices coming at him from all directions, male and female voices, all sharing the same hurried anxiety and panic. The tightness in his chest was excruciating, stealing his breath, hurting his head. He tried to open his eyes but it was as if his lids were held together with invisible thread. He wanted to tell them to find Mama and Papa. But his tongue had become trapped within his mouth and could not force the words from his sealed lips. Every breath he took hurt like needle pricks in his heart and soon a terrible numbness began to steal through his limbs. It had a chilly touch that reached into his body like icy fingers, numbing everything it touched. It rose from his toes, coursing through his knees, his thighs, his stomach....He knew that when it reached his heart he would die. He had been lucky so far not to have come to any harm in his night-flying. His mortal body would have died had anything happened to his spirit in its dark flights. But to survive the spirit world only to die unnecessarily before he had completed his mission was unbearable... so unfair. He did not want to die...*he did not want to die. Oh Jesus, please...*

The numbness crawled ever closer to his chest... nearer... tighter... and suddenly, he knew it was over. The impenetrable darkness once again drew him into its terrifying depths.

*****

He is running, panting, fleeing from the dark terror behind him. All around him are trees, great towering trees that steal the light from the bright moon in the dark skies. He doesn't know where he is but he knows who his pursuer is...he knows HER. *He hears her evil cackle as she bears down on him, snapping tree branches in her violent flight. He feels the hatred pouring from her like a living organism and he tries to run faster, to escape her claws. But his feet are weighted with rocks, sluggish, putting him in slow motion. She is fast gaining on him and soon, he knows he will join his ancestors on one of those lonely boulders in their water hell. He would rather die than become a Sad-man!* Oh Jesus! *Of course, he must die to become a Sad-man and then there will be no escape, ever.*

Just then, as he steels himself for death, he finds himself in a place that is as familiar as it is terrifying. Even before he hears their mournful wails or sees their hunched forms atop their rocky prisons, he knows he is back in the water-hell of his ancestors. And he can fly again, escaping the terror behind him. His entire body is pulsating with the familiar glow he recalls and strength flows back into his limbs. In the sudden brightness, he sees the Blood-man hunched on his solitary boulder, howling into his hands. Ikem bears down on him, his heart racing with fury and fear.

'It's your fault,' he screams at the Blood-man. 'It's all your fault! You sold her daughter and murdered her and now she wants to kill me too because of what you did. I hate you, I hate you. I hope you suffer forever and ever.' Hot tears cloud his vision and his body trembles with intense emotions. The rank stench of decay assails his nostrils but rage cloaks his senses from the foulness. The

Blood-man howls more intensely, bloody tears pouring from his empty sockets. He reaches out a blood-coated arm to Ikem - a pleading arm – but Ikem recoils from him, floating several feet away from his blood-drenched boulder.

'I am doomed,' the Blood-man wails, beating his head with his fists. 'We are all doomed. My child of Light; you are the only one that can save us. I know I deserve no mercy but have I not suffered enough? I lived to see the sudden deaths of all my twelve sons, even my eight grandsons before my death. And in every death, at each single burial, I beheld her gloating face. I thought that in death I would be free from her vengeance but I didn't know she had been a practiser of the dark arts. She used her evil powers to trap the souls of my sons in this water abyss, chained them to the one place they could never escape. She knew we are not water people, that our spirits can never traverse rivers and seas. I was as versed as her in the dark arts and would have resisted her curse in this realm. But what father can ignore the cries of his sons when he knows he is responsible for their plight? So, I stay here and mourn my sons and their sons and their sons' sons. Their innocent blood is on my head and my worthless body pours with their blood. Over days beyond the number of the stars have I begged for her forgiveness, praying for the day she will

finally set us free. My ancestors turn their backs on me for my despicable crime and will not intercede on my behalf. But they tell me that there is hope, that a child of light who bears her blood and my blood in his veins will come and set us free. You are our last hope, the impossible that yet is; my blood and her blood once again merged in a living son through some miracle I cannot fathom. Speak to her, our son. She will hear you... she must hear you...*for her blood courses through your veins.'*

Ikem stares in stunned disbelief at the Blood-man, unable to accept what his ears hear. How can he be related to the monstrous ghoul that has pursued him through the forest and into the dark realm of his ancestors' hell? How can he have the blood of that horror atop the palm-tree in his veins? Yet, something inside tells him the Blood-man speaks the truth. He remembers the young and beautiful woman he had mistaken for Mama's twin and knows she is truly his ancestor, just as the Blood-man is his ancestor. But the knowledge gives him no respite from his terror of the monster she has become.

Then he sees the Blood-man point to his left, towards a boulder set close to his own. Ikem's eyes follow the bloody finger and suddenly, his mouth opens in a piercing scream. For perched atop the new boulder is Papa...his Papa, wailing sadly into the night.

'Papa! Papa! Noo...oh Jesus! Egbawa o! *Help! nooo...' He flies to the boulder, struggling to perch on its wet surface. But the stone rejects his feet and he can only hover above it. Papa looks at him piteously, his eyes vacant like the rest of the Sad-men. And Ikem begins to howl, great sobs wracking his body, choking the breath from his lungs. Remembrance finally pierces through the dense fog of his mind - the harrowing drive up Milliken Hill, Papa's nightmare, the accident, the precipice...darkness.* Papa is dead. *His father is dead...dead. She has killed Papa as she's killed his ancestors. His Papa is now a Sad-man, a prisoner on an evil boulder in this horrible place.*

Seeing his once proud father reduced to the pathetic zombie on the huge rock kills something pure in Ikem's soul...his innocence, his childhood. He would rather die than let Papa suffer like this. If it kills him, he will set poor Papa free. The Blood-man says he can do it. So be it. He will confront the terrible hag and plead on their behalf.

Ikem turns and flies into the darkness. He has no idea where to find her but he knows that she'll find him, just as she's found him in the past. After all, she needs his soul to add to her trophy of the damned. He hears the wails of the Sad-men recede as he flies further and deeper into the night. Somewhere in that cacophony of pain is Papa's voice. A painful lump constricts his throat and his eyes burn behind his lids.

He smells her even before he hears that terrible cackle. It is a pungent smell of decay and corruption, blood and death. He knows she has found him, seen his glow. He resists the burning urge to flee, to fly back to the water-hell of his ancestors...anywhere that will shield him from this terrible harbinger of death. His heart is pounding furiously, so loud he can hear it through the harsh gasps of his breathing. But the memory of Papa's lost face stills his flight and he turns to face the foulest of his nightmares.

She is before him, right in front of him. His courage deserts him as he opens his mouth to scream at the unspeakable horror he sees. But his lips are as frozen as his limbs and he can only stare at the evil that has pursued him through the endless night. And it is a terrible sight to behold, worse than what he had witnessed above the Palm-tree. On that occasion, he could still see the vestiges of the young and tragic woman he had believed to be his mother's twin. The black mangled creature with scaly skin and taloned hands he now beholds can no longer be considered human in any form, spirit or flesh. The twisted and fetid body is straight out of the worst nightmare of every human, young and old. Instinctively, he shuts his eyes, unwilling to see his own death.

Then he hears a voice behind him, a voice that floods his entire body with relief, joy - Mama's voice, loud and strong in the deep night. He opens his eyes and turns to flee into her arms. What he sees stuns him. Mama is flying; and just like him, she is glowing, pulsating with a light that rivals the blaze of the sun. She appears nude yet he is unable to see any part of her body beneath the blinding shimmer of her aura. He flies into her arms, holding her tight, a small child once again, his arms like pincers around her waist. He feels her warmth and her strength and it heals his fear, but not all of it. He sees the scaly horror pause, poised between puzzle and indecision. Its canine-sharp teeth are barred and its eyes blaze more fiercely than ever. The sight fills him with terror once again and he clings even tighter to Mama. Mama holds him briefly then gently pushes him aside. She flies towards the hag, her glowing body a shield between him and his hunter.

'You will not take my son.' Mama shouts at the horror, her voice strong, fearless. It brings a startle to the hag's face, which rapidly turns into a thunderous scowl.

'Woman! Do you dare challenge me?' It roars, its voice a hollow boom that layers his skin with goosebumps. 'Move aside before I dispatch you to your ancestors. The boy's soul is mine, like the soul of every male that shares the same bloodline as Ezeoha Ani. Do not interfere with

issues that are no concern of yours. Go now or die with your precious son.' Its voice shakes the dark skies and thunder booms in the air, bringing a great wind that churns the waters below, pushing against Mama.

But Mama is filled with the fierce resolve of a true mother and will not budge.

'Nne, you will not harm my son,' Mama repeats, her voice now soft, even gentle. The creature rushes forward, its talons reaching for Mama's throat. Ikem screams and flies to her aid, fury and fear aiding his flight. He will not let it kill Mama as it has killed Papa. It will have to kill him first. He sees the terrible claws on Mama's throat and hears the stunned hiss of the creature as it quickly withdraws its claws. The air sizzles with the smell of burnt flesh and Mama holds him firmly against her body.

'Nne, I beg you to pause and look at me.' Mama's voice is still that gentle cajoling pitch that leaves him perplexed. Why does she talk to the monster as if it is her own child; the same hag that has just tried to kill her? *'Nne, please...look through the cloak of your hate and see me...really see me. Can't you see that I am you as you once were? Can't you see your daughter, Ndidi, in my face?' Mama's voice is choked and he feels her tears wet his skin.*

The creature pauses, stunned. Its face contorts in a mixture of shock and disbelief. Uncertainty layers its terrible pupils as it slowly lowers its arms. It glides closer to Mama... slowly...its movements hesitant like a trapped beast, wary and uncertain. It stops and peers into Mama's face, long and hard. Its breath is rancid and hot but Mama does not flinch.

'Your daughter, Ndidi, did not perish at the hands of the slave-traders all those centuries ago.' Mama's voice is almost a whisper. 'Their leader decided to marry her rather than sell her off to the White men. As a result, her children and their descendants, myself included, have since been from the Yoruba tribe. I never knew of our link to Ezeoha Ani when I married his ancestor, also named after him. All I knew was that my husband was an Igbo man, a kind and wonderful doctor who loved my family as if they were his own. And now, you have taken him away from me.' Mama's voice breaks and her tears flow faster. Her arm tightens around Ikem and he struggles to hold back his own tears. Papa! *Proud and kind Papa! He'll never see Papa again, not in the human realm, unless he joins him on one of those evil boulders if this vengeful demon gets its way. The creature is hissing and snarling, trying to reach out for Ikem. But it is unable to pierce through the protective light of his aura. Mama's face twists in a sad smile.*

'Nne, you will not take my son as you have taken his father because just like your daughter, Ndidi, Ezeoha's blood and your blood flow through his veins. By a strange twist of fate, destiny brought me and Ezeoha together, uniting that which had been broken through the centuries by the dastardly act of one man. You and Ezeoha are both our ancestors and my son is the only living male that bears both your bloodlines. So you will not harm us...you cannot *harm us...for to harm us is to destroy yourself. We are protected by your blood which runs in our veins.' Mama pauses and then stretches out her right arm to the creature. 'Nne...Great-mother, we have returned to you. Won't you welcome us home?'*

The creature stares at Mama's outstretched arm, then turns its fearsome gaze at Ikem. He tries to hold her gaze but his courage deserts him like smoke caught in a whirlwind. He shuts his eyes.

Then he hears a shriek that nearly voids his bladder. Mama gasps. His eyes fly open and he too gasps. The creature is in manic flight, flinging itself with violent force against several tree branches. Its howls fill the air, a sound full of fury and pain. Mama holds him close, his ears pressed to her chest. He hears the loud thudding of her heart. It mimics his own heart.

A sudden silence descends and Ikem lifts his head. The creature is staring at them, its fury spent. It glides towards them and Ikem tightens his grip on Mama's waist, his shoulders tense. The creature pauses a few inches from Mama and again stares at her for several tense minutes. It stretches a tentative hand to Mama's face, its movements unsure, like a wild dog offered food by human hands. Ikem waits for the contact to burn its flesh as before. Nothing happens. Its flesh does not sizzle. He feels a great terror constrict his heart. Their protection is gone! The dreadful creature has broken through the shield of their aura!

He starts to pull Mama back, away from the hag. Then he stops, transfixed by what he sees. A dramatic change is taking place in the creature. Right before his eyes, its pupils begin to lose the fearsome bloodiness that petrifies his soul. Its eyes begin to fill up, this time with real clear water - human tears. They spill over and drench her face. She covers her face with her hands and moans. Her body quakes with a deep sorrow borne over several centuries. Mama stretches a comforting hand to her shoulder. She looks up at them with eyes free of hate, her pupils soft and sad.

Through her scars and disfigurement, Ikem finally sees the true face of Mama's great ancestor as she had once been before Ezeoha, the Blood-man, ruined her life with his cruel brutality. Her skin is still coated with the hard scales that deny her humanity and her head bears the bloody gore of her death-blows. But the vile stench that follows her like maggots to a putrid corpse is gone and Ikem can breathe without gagging.

'My daughter! My daughter!' Nne cups Mama's cheek, rubbing her flesh, her movements gentle, tender. Tears are still streaming down her face and Ikem knows they are tears of joy. She enfolds Mama in her arms, holding on to her as if she will never let go. Mama is also crying and he feels a hard lump in his throat. Then he remembers Papa, poor Papa, trapped in that cold, dark water-hell with the Sad-men. His tears spill in a bitter pool.

'Mama, tell her to let Papa go,' he cries, shaking Mama's arm, his voice urgent. He sees a scowl descend on his great ancestor's face and once again he fears her wrath. But Mama is still wrapped in her arms, her face blissful and full of peace. The look makes him angry. A sense of betrayal fills his heart with bitterness. Mama has no business being so happy with someone that has killed her husband and almost killed her son. He tugs her arm again, this time more violently.

'Mama, tell her to let Papa go. Tell her now,' his voice is loud, angry. Mama turns to him and she sees his

pain. She places a gentle hand on his hair and turns to their great ancestor.

'Nne, great-mother, please hear the pleas of this child, your son,' Mama's voice is the same voice that good mothers all over the world sooth their crying babies with - gentle and tender. 'Ndidi knows that you have avenged her betrayal and punished those that stole your life from you so brutally and wickedly. But it is now time for you to rest. Our people have a saying which I'm sure you remember; the jailor is as much a prisoner as the prisoner. *So I beseech you great-mother, set them free so that you too will be free. For the sake of this child - my son - who carries your blood in his veins, please set his father and the rest of his ancestors free.'*

Ikem feels Mama's hand on his shoulders, urging him forward towards his great ancestor. And this time, he goes willingly for he sees that the danger has gone.

'Speak to Nne,' Mama says to him, her voice hushed. 'Plead your case before her and atone for your ancestors' crimes. Don't be afraid, my son. Everything will be okay'

He swallows, his heart beginning to race again. What should he say? Where does he start? Everyone's fate rests on him and he doesn't want to mess things up. Suddenly, he hears the Blood-man's voice in his head, strong and clear - "speak to her. She will hear you; she MUST hear you, for you are the impossible that yet is."

His fears disappear. He realises that there are no right or wrong words. Anything he says will be right because it is as it is destined to be. A person can never escape their fate.

'Nne, please forgive them,' his voice rings out in the intense silence of the night. 'They're very sorry for what they did to you and I am also very sorry for what they did and I wish Ezeoha will suffer forever for what he did to you because any father that sells their child should burn in hell forever and..'

'Ikem!' Mama's scandalised shout cuts him off as she pushes him away. 'You are supposed to make things better, not worse.' She turns to Nne. 'Great-mother, please ignore what the boy said. He's only a child and knows no better. He's just worried about his father, that's all.' Mama's face is anxious, pleading.

To his shock, he hears his great ancestor laugh! It is a loud laugh, a real laugh, an indulgent laugh. Gone is the hideous cackle of his nightmare. When she turns to him, her face is wreathed in smiles. She stretches out her arm and pats his head.

'The child speaks the truth, for children lack the subterfuge of their elders,' she says, her voice tinged with

sadness. 'Ezeoha and his son and kinsmen deserve to rot for eternity in the same waters they sold my daughter into. But you're right...' Nne pauses and heaves a deep sigh. 'It is time to let the others go. Except that to free one soul, I must free the whole. The curse was on the house of Ezeoha and all his male descendants. Still...I guess it matters nought now that I know the truth and you are returned to me.' Her shoulders lift in a weary shrug. She turns back to Mama. 'You have to return to Etiti, to Ezeoha's hamlet. Find the great Iroko tree there and dig beneath it. The tree still stands today even though the huts are gone. My bones are buried beneath that tree. They dug my body up and buried me beneath that tree after the death of Ezeoha's first son, Obinna. Ezeoha thought his shrine would hold my spirit; that his personal chi *was stronger than mine. But he was wrong.' A hard smile fleets over her face and Ikem shivers. He knows the tiger still lurks beneath the kitten and its claws could sharpen at any time. 'Go. Find my bones and bury me in clean soil, free from the evil of that accursed tree. My fight with that shrine has been a long and hard one and I have not emerged unscathed.' She takes a long deep breath and places a gentle hand on Mama's right cheek. Ikem marvels yet again at the uncanny resemblance between them in spite of her ghastly appearance. 'My daughter, don't forget to speak the final rites over my bones, the rites my Ndidi would have spoken for me had she been there when I died. The boy must speak the rites of blessing, of penitence and forgiveness, as he is the one that bears the joint blood of Ezeoha and I.' She leans forward to hug Mama long and hard, before enfolding Ikem in her embrace.*

He stiffens, prepared to hold his breath, a part of him still frightened despite all the changes and revelations. But the stench is gone and her touch fills him with an unexpected peace that brings the moisture to his eyes.

'Hurry, child,' she whispers into his ears, her voice sounding far, faint, like a sigh in the wind. 'Hurry... for I can scarcely wait for my release. Hurry...hurry...'

*****

'Hurry! Call the doctor! The child is awake at last!' Ikem heard the words as he awoke to see the smiling face of a white-clad nurse. He tried to smile but his skin felt like plastic, hard and tight. But he must have done well, for the nurse's smile broadened. She stooped to pat his head.

'You're fine now, Ikem. You're okay now, child. Just relax and doctor will be with you shortly. Just don't fall back to sleep, okay? Keep your eyes wide open…that's it…just like that, good boy.' She raised both her arms to the air, her eyes briefly closed. 'Thank you, Jesus! God is great!' She turned her smiling gaze back to him. '*Chei!* You have no idea how much you frightened us! You are truly a miracle boy that have come back from the grave! Alleluia! Our God is truly a mighty God!'

'Mama…' His voice sounded like a frog's croak to his ears. He coughed out a lump in his throat. 'Mama…Papa…'

He saw an anxious look flash over the nurse's face - unease, uncertainty.

'Your mummy's just fine. She's in the room next to yours. Don't worry. If you keep getting stronger and better, you'll be able to see your mummy very soon, okay?' She looked at the open door of his room, the anxious look on her face relaxing to a smile of relief as the doctor walked in, flanked by more nurses. Ikem shut his eyes, trying to shut out the sudden pounding pain in his head. He felt like an old man of forty instead of the thirteen year old boy he was. He felt the doctor's warm hand on his forehead, his wrist; felt the hard coldness of the stethoscope on his bare chest. Hands prised his lids apart but his eyes were too weary to stay open.

In the darkness of his world, he felt a sudden peace descend on him, a peace such as he'd not had since the first time he met the Blood-man in the place of eternal darkness all those years ago. Images flashed through his mind and vivid thoughts began to fill in the gaps in his memory. Recollecting his encounters with his great ancestors, he now knew with the certainty of Jesus' resurrection that his A*mosu* days were over. Together, he and Mama would carry out the wishes of Great-mother Nne, she who had finally forgiven, before returning to Lagos. Papa and his dead ancestors would at last be at rest. He didn't need the nurse to tell him that Papa was dead. Her silence confirmed what he had already witnessed in that dark water-hell of his ancestors.

Ikem felt warm tears dampen his cheeks. Grandmama Modupe had been right about towns. They will either accept you or reject you. If only he'd made a fuss much earlier when he'd first felt the rejection of Enugu town, maybe things would have turned out differently. But perhaps, as his Grandmama Modupe always said, *"no one can change the lines of their palms. A man's future lies in his own hands. In the end, everyone must live out their destiny.*"

THE NAMES OF OUR DEAD

'Why was everyone dying? They had all been so alive just yesterday.'

(Yoko Ogawa – Revenge)

I

There is an obscure village to the south of mine called Okwukwe, the land of Hope. Less than two hours trek from us, Okwukwe is famed for its monthly market. My village, Ngwo, is set above the famous Milliken Hill, named after the White colonial engineer that supervised the construction of the winding road that snakes down it. Milliken's road connects my village to the rest of the neighbouring towns.

It is said that during its construction, over one hundred able-bodied braves at the peak of their manhood, lost their lives on the job. The elders said they were either mauled by the wild beasts that were abound in the mountains in those days or crushed to death by the heavy boulders they had to log up the treacherous slopes. It is said that all the dead, to the last man, were from my village, Ngwo.

I remember our teacher, Agu, telling our class about the fire snake, which was longer than a python, gulping down black coal for its meal, eternally hungry. Agu said that Milliken's road had been built for the fire snake, which was coming to our village to devour the children that wouldn't go to the missionary school to learn the ways of the White man. The fire snake eventually came on its metal path, but not to our village. I've never ridden in it but the twin brothers, Sunday and Monday, made the ride from Kafanchan. They never completed the journey, though. They said they had jumped out of the fire-demon because of what - or rather - *who* they had seen inside its dark bowels. The twins said they had seen Ozo, seated in his old splendour, towards the front of the train - Ozo, our bravest and strongest, our pride and glory in the days of my childhood; Ozo who had died dumb, blind and broken, a victim of his own pride and folly.

II

It is said that in the days after the construction of Milliken's road, travellers would frequently report macabre sightings and gourd-cracking wails from the depths of the surrounding gorge. Many accidents happened on that road and people died like flies in a weekly occurrence, which soon gained it the name, *Death Route*. Yet, not a single soul from my village ever died on Milliken's road. I remember my father recounting the story of the mini wagon that had tumbled into the deepest part of the gorge, with all thirty souls aboard. All had died, except the three men from my village. They came out of the mangled bus, dazed but unscathed. They told how they had been borne on strong and loving arms, shrouded in mist and fog. They said the spectres, clothed in red raffia and beads, the traditional costume of my village, had carried them from the mangled wreck of the wagon, littered with the corpses of the other passengers, in a single file of silent tribute. As they were gently laid to safety on the asphalt top of Milliken's road, their rescuers had uttered a single word in unison, before making their floating retreat to the depths of the gorge. They had said *'De-eje,'* the language of my people, meaning 'peace,' 'welcome.'

Maá, our witch-doctor, spoke to the night. His gong rang out eerily in the middle of our sleep to tell us what we already suspected. Our saviours were our sons, our dead braves, sacrificed for the sake of Mr Milliken's infamous road.

III

Mr Milliken's road saw an increase in traffic through my village, especially on that Eke market day when the obscure village, Okwukwe, opened its market to the world. Yet, even though the towns around us visited Okwukwe each month and the village was less than two hours trek from us, nobody from my village ever patronised that famed market. In our known history, only five people had ever gone there.

The first was Nwoga, the tobacco seller, who became cursed by the gods after visiting Okwukwe market. She was brought back, a gibberish bundle of supreme lunacy, unable to utter a single intelligible word. Eventually, she needed to be restrained with ropes tied to a metal post, to prevent her stripping and inflicting harm on herself and others. Nwoga eventually choked herself to death with a handful of pebbles, a sad pitiful mockery of what had once been a striking village girl of unsurpassed beauty.

It is told that the next person to visit Okwukwe from my village was a man called Ngwu, at the time, the owner of the largest yam barn in our village. They say Ngwu was a successful farmer and a prominent son of the community. Yet, he went to Okwukwe despite the entreaties of his wives and daughters… or perhaps, as some people have implied, *because* of the entreaties of his wives and daughters. He had returned from Okwukwe vacant eyed and dazed. He committed suicide that same day without ever uttering a single word.

I heard from my father that Israel, the educated and much travelled star of our village, was the third victim of

Okwukwe. Israel worked with the White colonial masters at the seaside town of Onitsha. He could speak English from the nose, just like the White man. It was rumoured that the White masters planned to send Israel to visit their King in London as a reward for his loyalty and brilliance. Israel was also a Christian. He did not believe in the stupid village superstition about Okwukwe. So, he went to Okwukwe to prove a civilised point.

He returned alive. But he never went to London to visit the king. He never went anywhere else. Israel is now the village idiot. I see him most days. He is an old man with spittle dripping down the sides of his mouth, as he laughs or cries alternatively in his pitiful stupidity.

Our chief, Igwe, is perhaps the most famous victim of Okwukwe because his fate was unlike that of the others. My father told me Igwe had gone to solve the mystery of Okwukwe once and for all and bring back sanity to the village. The speculations in Ngwo at the time were utterly destructive to the morale of our people. Before he left for Okwukwe, Maá, our witch-doctor, fortified our chief with amulets and charms and the blessings of our ancestors.

I remember that Igwe left us, amidst great pomp, fear and hope. There was dancing and singing, feasting and drinking throughout the day preceding his departure. That was the last he was seen. Igwe never came back to us again.

No word was heard from him, ever. Igwe disappeared as if he had never walked the land of our fathers. For a long time, our villagers wandered aimlessly, confused and helpless, like children abandoned by their mother. I remember seeing the adults then, hurdled in groups, always talking in hushed tones, their faces grim and sombre. Speculation was rife, accusations, strong. The men were for outright war against Okwukwe. The women, fearful for their children, preached caution.

And in the midst of all the confusion, stood out one figure - Ozo the Brave, who had led our warriors in the twelve hours war against the insulting Nkanu tribe; Ozo the strong, who had single-handedly dispatched six Nkanu warriors to their ancestor's hell; Ozo the tall, towering at over six feet seven; Ozo the beautiful, whose melodious voice and piercing eyes beneath bushy brows, could bring the moist heat to the thighs of every village woman under the age of toothless grin; Ozo, who was to become the last and most poignant victim of the Okwukwe tragedy.

IV

I still remember the terrible events that had followed the disappearance of our chief Igwe, fifty-six years ago, even though I was a mere boy of ten years in those days. A few weeks after Igwe disappeared, the villagers lynched Maá, for failing to provide adequate protection to our lost chief. They said his juju medicine had soured. He had been stingy with his sacrifices to the ancestors and as a result, they had abandoned our innocent chief in his hour of need. If only we'd known what we now know, we would have realised that no charm made by man would have protected our beloved chief from the terrible curse of Okwukwe.

Maá's shrine was burnt to the ground by the enraged villagers, achieving with one fateful stroke, what the missionaries had failed to achieve in decades of rice and prayers. In those days, rice was a delicacy used by the missionaries to bribe us to the Christian faith. It soon became the Sunday food for the villagers, who would rush to church to eat the delicacy and sing the White man's songs, before rushing back to offer the saved rice to the shrines of the ancestors. The burning of Maá's shrine marked the end of the concerted worship of the ancestors in our village.

As the men demanded vengeance against Okwukwe, feverish preparations were made for this crucial war. Ozo tried to bring calm to a hysterical village. He encouraged the men to complete the ploughing of the farms and the planting of yams and cassava tubers, to ensure the women and children did not starve should their men fall in the battleground of Okwukwe. Ozo supervised the repairs of the thatched roofs of the red mud huts, as well as the tarring of the grounds of the village square for the forthcoming "*Odo Masquerade*" festival.

Then, in a final stroke of statesmanship, Ozo volunteered to reconnoitre the enemy territory before leading his men to the battlefront. We all knew Ozo was a warrior and a fighter, unlike the others that had gone before him. Yet, everyone tried to dissuade him from taking such a risky journey alone. But Ozo was resolute in his determination. He was a proud warrior and would not be accused of cowardice. In his pride and confidence, Ozo failed to make adequate preparations for his wives and children, certain that he would return to set his house in order before leaving for war and the total annihilation of the Okwukwe indigenes for good.

And so it was that Ozo left our village in the deep of night amidst silent embraces and handclasps by his comrades-in-arms, in marked contrast to the fanfare that had accompanied the departure of our lost chief. Only the men saw Ozo leave, though the women and we children knew about his journey. But we spoke no word about it, in case the owl, that bird of ill-omen, heard us and carried the news to the Okwukwe people.

Ozo was gone for two nights and on the third day, he returned to our village, expected but unheralded. For, the first sight of his countenance, cast the dark cloak of terror on the entire village. Ozo looked like a man that had stared the cold mask of death in the face and lived to tell the tale. I remember that I was outside catching grasshoppers with my cousins in the bushy landscape of our compound, when we heard the commotion from the village square. We joined the rush of human stream flowing towards the square, where we heard talk that Ozo was seated in splendour.

It was a lie. Ozo was neither seated nor cloaked in splendour. Instead, I saw him leaning against the shoulder of his younger brother, Ude, haunted eyes staring out of a gaunt face, suddenly aged beyond belief in the space of three days. His legs looked as if they could barely support his huge frame and his right arm jerked spasmodically, as if pulled by a puppet master's strings. The crowds that had gathered to cheer stared awe-stricken, unable to offer the mandatory '*De-eje*' welcome salutation of our tribe. We all waited in sweaty suspense, willing Ozo to speak. For we could see from the taut look on his face that his mouth strained to unchain his tongue and spill out his tale. Nobody doubted the news would be terrible, not after seeing Ozo as he had looked on that fateful day.

Finally, using the last of his immense strength to pull himself to an upright position, Ozo raised his undamaged left arm for silence and at last, began to speak. At the beginning, he seemed to stumble over his words, sounding almost as gibberish as Israel the Idiot that many feared for his sanity. Then suddenly, strength, clarity and volume were restored to his voice as if by a magic hand. And Ozo, once again the powerful orator, began to unfold the dreadful mystery of Okwukwe to the horror-stricken villagers.

Ozo spoke for over an hour, standing tall and proud as was ever his way. And then, at the end of his long speech, he slumped and fell against his brother, whose inferior strength could not break the great fall of this giant Iroko tree, King of Trees. As the villagers surged as one to help our fallen hero, he shook his head violently, as if trying to clear an invisible fog that had blanketed his vision. He made a grunting sound like one in great pain, and slumped, unconscious. My mother, like the rest of the women, hurriedly shepherded us children into the safety of our huts, to await with unmasked terror, the return of our men. And when my father returned, his news struck an even deeper chord of fear in us. Ozo the brave, the strong, the beautiful, had been struck lame, blind and dumb!

I saw him a few times before his death and was struck with immense sadness at the destruction of what was once, our greatest and our best. The whites of his once piercing eyes stared vacantly into nothingness; his mouth moved convulsively, but no sounds would ever come from those lips again. His once mighty and muscular frame would never be borne upright by strong sturdy legs. That huge but fast-dilapidating body trembled and shook like the wind-tossed leaf of a mango tree. The saddest part of the tragedy was that, unlike Israel, Ozo's brain and faculties remained intact. He could still supervise the cultivation and harvesting of his large cassava farms, advising with hand signs, the quantity of tubers to be planted and the timing of the harvesting. He still managed the finances as the head of his family and his children never lacked food, or his wives, clothes. The messengers of Okwukwe had left him alive but physically ruined, as a constant reminder and a final warning to a proud and stubborn people - my people.

Now, we are tamed. We finally know the truth and our curiosity is cured. Nobody from Ngwo even dreams of visiting that accursed land, Okwukwe. Ozo, like others before him, except Israel our village idiot, is finally dead, at least, to us. The twins, Sunday and Monday, claim to have seen him in the bowels of the fire-demon from Kanfanchan and we believe them. We have to, because we know the truth now. The terrible secret of Okwukwe lies in the speech Ozo made on that fateful day.

And now, I leave the contents of his speech as a warning to our children, the future generation, whose arrogance, born from the White man's teachings, may yet be their doom should they ignore the lessons of our past.

"Brothers, I bring you this message from the land of Okwukwe. I alone have lived to tell this tale because I have been spared by the messengers, to ensure that their orders are obeyed. But to them I shall return when my days on this earth are done. For none who ventures to Okwukwe from Ngwo, can ever be restored to the bosoms of our ancestors.

Hear and heed this today! Any son or daughter of Ngwo who visits Okwukwe, should be certain of one thing - Death! Okwukwe is for all, except the children of Ngwo. The people of Okwukwe want to be left alone. Brothers, they have paid their dues but their memories are long. Their thoughts are warped and their souls are still as dark as ever. I am instructed to name some of the messengers to you, because you know them all, by name and by face, and you will pay heed to their warning. The messengers I met at Okwukwe were, Eze, Okwo, Ani, Ngwu, Oji, Nwoga, Onoh, Igwe, Ugwu, Nde, Nuzo, Nude, Ukwuani..."

V

I remember that as Ozo reeled out the names impassively, a great cry was let out in the square. The women fled in panic, children in hand, while some dropped in dead faints, even before Ozo himself collapsed. Others shrieked in terror and pressed their palms against their ears to keep out the horror. The men clenched weakened fists in an attempt to prevent the cowardly piss of abject terror.

For all the names that Ozo called out in his sad, yet, ominous voice that summer's day in our village square, were the names of our own; the names of our dead! They were names that in their lifetime, inspired terror and hate in the hearts of our people - murderers, serial and sadistic rapists, slave-traders, child-stealers and genital mutilators, night-flyers, who stole the souls of the strongest and bravest in their innocent slumber, witches and conjurers, shape-changers and bloodsuckers, poisoners and betrayers, mystically-endowed albinos and dwarves! They were the reviled citizens of Ngwo, whose bodies rotted in unhallowed grounds at the outskirts of the village, bound and chained with powerful charms to keep their vengeful spirits at bay. Frustrated parents still threaten wayward children with their nightmare-inducing names and the

Christian converts still cross themselves when they walk past their graves.

Today, Okwukwe still thrives as a busy market village, where everything can be bought for a lark. And even though the towns around us visit Okwukwe each month and the village is less than two hours trek from us, we, the indigenes of Ngwo, have finally turned our backs on it.

Milton Keynes UK
Ingram Content Group UK Ltd.
UKHW010644021023
429777UK00001B/1